PARANORMAL MYSTERY

Carols & Yule Perils

TRIXIE SILVERTALE

Sittin' On A Goldmine
Productions L.L.C.

Sittin' On A Goldmine Productions, L.L.C.

info@sittinonagoldmine.co

www.sittinonagoldmine.co

Publisher's note: This is a work of fiction. Names, characters, places and incidents are products of the author's imagination or are used fictitiously and are not to be construed as real. Any resemblance to actual events, locales, organizations, or persons, living or dead, is entirely coincidental.

ISBN: 978-0-9998758-8-9

Cover Design © Sittin' On A Goldmine Productions, L.L.C.

Trixie Silvertale
Carols and Yule Perils: Paranormal Cozy Mystery : a novel / by Trixie Silvertale — 1st ed.
[1. Paranormal Cozy Mystery — Fiction. 2. Cozy Mystery — Fiction. 3. Amateur Sleuths — Fiction. 4. Female Sleuth — Fiction. 5. Wit and Humor — Fiction.] 1. Title.

CHAPTER 1

NEVER IN ALL my Arizona-born days did I imagine myself trudging through knee-deep snow in almost-Canada to cut down my very own Christmas tree! But, as I prepare to celebrate my second Christmas in Pin Cherry Harbor, the place I now call home, I'm distracted by my job as a human snowplow.

To be honest, I've grown to love this place in a way I never thought possible, but I'm still not a huge fan of snow.

However, this hike does have an upside. The view!

Leading the way toward Birch County's secret stash of perfect Christmas trees is Sheriff Erick Harper.

He's marching along as though he was born to it, and he makes wading through two feet of snow with a chainsaw look like a Paris runway during fashion week.

As my newly acquired boots break through the crust of snow and sink into the powder beneath, the distance between my warm-hearted boyfriend and me grows with each step.

He stops, glances over his shoulder, and his sky-blue eyes dance with mischief. "You okay back there, Moon?"

"Don't get smart, Sheriff. I don't have quite as many years of experience hiking through the snow as you do."

I feel like a snowwoman suddenly exposed to the direct heat of the sun when his lips curve in an enticing grin. "Are you calling me an old man?"

While Erick may be five years older than me, he's far from an old man. His broad shoulders tower above me and a swath of his beautiful blond bangs slips out from beneath his beanie.

"Not old. Let's call it seasoned." I smirk and shrug.

He howls with laughter and strides off toward a stand of prized balsam fir. "You should've tried the snowshoes. I'm telling you, it's ten times easier."

Easier! He thinks that strapping some contraptions that look like tennis rackets to the feet of a naturally clumsy person, and then sending that person into the wild to trip over their own *feet-*

rackets is somehow a solution. You gotta love this guy.

As I continue slogging through the deep drifts, the antique mood ring on my left hand sizzles out a warning. Pretending to stop and tie my snow boots —not sure if that's even a thing—I slip off my mitten and sneak a peek. Something red—

Erick comes to a sudden halt, drops the chainsaw, and shouts, "Stay where you are, Moon."

It's so cute that he thinks he can command me. I dig deep into my young but uncooperative body and *run* to his side.

He shakes his head in dismay and raises a finger to his lips.

Before he has a chance to bring me up to speed, I whisper, "Is that blood in the snow?"

He nods. "I think it is. Probably a wounded animal. Hopefully a rabbit or fox, but if it's a wolf, that could be dangerous. I'm gonna hustle back to the cruiser and grab my sidearm."

"10-4."

Erick ignores my attempt to play deputy. "Stay still and quiet."

While he lopes away as though he's traversing a grassy meadow rather than plowing through months of snowfall, a sudden realization hits me.

I'm alone in the woods!

Sure, I have a chainsaw, but I don't know how

to use it. There's probably an injured timber wolf stalking me at this very moment. Goodbye, Sweet Erick. Who knows what might've been?

The once inviting forest shifts, as the leafless birch trees take on the appearance of skeletons clawing into the air, and the green of the dark pines becomes an ominous black.

Sitting in the profound silence, my brain kicks into overdrive with operation: Distract Mitzy from Sudden Death.

Somehow the thick layer of snow sucks all sound from the air. It's like the world's best sound-dampening blanket. If I could figure out a way to manufacture something with this level of sound absorption, maybe I could turn my clichéd film-school dropout story into an inspirational inventor's TED talk.

The sharp call of a reddish-pink bird with grey wings echoes through the forest, and my clairaudience unfortunately deciphers the song.

Death. Death. Death.

Before I can scream with the ferocity of a horror-movie scream queen, Erick's tramping return snaps me out of my psychic panic.

He takes one look at my face, draws his weapon, and cocks it. "Did you see a wolf?"

I have to tell him . . . And I pray he doesn't ask

too many questions. "It's not a wolf. I think it might be a human."

His head tilts to one side. "One of your hunches?"

I nod.

Adopting a tactical crouch, he follows the blood trail.

Plodding along behind, I'm hoping the freezing temperatures have thrown my extrasensory perceptions off and all we find is an injured, but still alive, bunny.

No such luck.

Twenty feet ahead of us, on the rough trail, is a crumpled pile of winter gear and boots. I know there's a human in there somewhere.

He holsters his weapon and rushes forward.

The stark pool of red in the alabaster snow is all I need to see. My clairsentience gives me an additional punch in the gut, whether or not I want it.

She's dead.

Erick rolls her over, and from a tiny hole in the front of her neon-blue jacket . . . blooms red death.

You'd think I'd be used to it by now, but it gets me every time. I run off the trail, grip the black-and-white scarred trunk of a birch, and unload my breakfast in a most unladylike fashion.

When I return to the trail, Erick is on the phone, trying to call for backup deputies and the medical examiner. "I can't get a solid signal out here. I should run back to the cruiser and call this in. Do you want to stay or go?"

Keeping my distance, I avert my gaze and blow out a shaky breath.

"I'm not sure what to say, Moon. I know I tease you about being a corpse magnet, but this is uncanny."

I hate when he uses the word uncanny. It's easy to sense he has suspicions about my hunches. While he knows I can see ghosts, I haven't been completely honest with him about my psychic powers. "Why is it so *uncanny*?"

"Well, you know, we parked at Twiggy's cabin and she gave us permission to cut a tree or two on her property, and this woman—"

"Is it Twiggy? It can't be. She was at the bookshop when we left." My extrasensory perceptions have completely checked out. No help at all. I can't afford to lose my one and only employee! Especially not one who works for nothing but front-row seats to my unavoidable klutzdom!

"It's not Twiggy. It's Carol Olsen."

I look at Erick as though he's crazy and throw my hands in the air. "Is that name supposed to mean something to me?"

He steps away from the body and exhales as he

approaches me. "You know the guy Twiggy's on-again/off-again dating?"

Swallowing loudly, I struggle to find my voice. "Wayne?"

Erick jerks a thumb over his shoulder toward the body. "That's his ex-wife."

CHAPTER 2

NOW THAT WE have stumbled upon a crime scene, Erick is hesitant to leave the body unattended. Being an amazing girlfriend, I step up to the plate and offer to head back to the cabin and call the station.

A few hours earlier, I would've thought nothing about wandering alone through this idyllic winter wonderland. Of course, after our discovery, my mind works overtime playing tricks on me, and I think I'm seeing a murderer behind every tree.

When I approach the lone cabin in the woods, the "Gone Fishing" doormat peeks out from under a layer of snow and strikes me as a sad epitaph for the recently departed Carol Olsen. The two-bedroom clapboard structure sits quietly amidst the deep drifts of the long winter pressing against its lake-facing side. Of course, said lake is a frozen tundra at present.

Luckily, I've been to Twiggy's woodland outpost once before. If I needed to psychically replay the memory of how to light pilot lights and open fireplace flues to set up the cabin for habitation, I could. But I only need to ignore the musty abandoned smell, and make a couple of phone calls.

First: Call the station to request backup, and tell them to get the medical examiner into the office on a Sunday.

Second: Call my dad. Not because I need comfort or anything like that. I simply want a ride home.

If Erick had driven his personal vehicle out here, he might've let me drive it back, but there's absolutely no way he's handing over the keys to his county-issued vehicle to a civilian.

Both calls go off without a hitch, and I promise to fill my dad in on all the details on our drive back to Pin Cherry.

The deputies are the first to arrive, lights flashing and sirens blaring. While there isn't exactly an emergency, they don't see a lot of action in our tiny town, so any excuse to put the pedal to the metal is eagerly accepted.

My father, Jacob Duncan, fruit of the loins of

my grandmother's third marriage, arrives a few minutes later. "Hey, Dad."

As a reformed felon who did hard time, he's a quick study. He glances at the two patrol cars and runs a worried hand through his white-blond hair. Intelligent grey eyes, which are a mirror of my own, widen, and one corner of his mouth tugs upward. "I'm gonna go out on a limb here. Is it a body?"

Playfully pushing him back toward his 1950s Ford pickup truck, I grumble under my breath. "Between you and Erick, I've had about all the wisecracks I can take for one day. I can't help it if I happened to be walking through an area where a crime was committed. It's not my fault. Certainly not my choice. And it's definitely not uncanny!"

Jacob opens the door for me and pats me on the back as I climb in. "And I'm the Queen of Sheba." He slams the door and his shoulders shake with laughter as he walks to the driver's side.

I cross my arms and pretend to pout while he powers through the deep snow and heads toward the main road.

"So, am I gonna have to pry this story out of you with french fries, or are you gonna volunteer it?"

My stomach is still a little swirly from the *discovery*. Despite my love of—some would say obsession with—fries, the thought does not sit well. "I'll tell you anything you want to know. Just don't make me eat."

Concern fills his gaze, and he eases off the gas. "Do you need to go to the hospital? I didn't mean to poke fun if you're really not feeling well."

"No. No, you're fine. I tossed my cookies earlier when we found—"

"So it is a body?"

I nod, yank my stocking hat off my head, and wipe the clammy sweat from my brow. "Yeah. We were headed out to cut a Christmas tree for the bookshop and one for Erick's house— Shoot! Now he's not gonna have a tree."

My dad reaches his strong hand toward me and pats my knee. "Don't you think he'd rather spend Christmas with us? Last week you told me his mother was heading to Florida to visit her sister for the holidays. Even if he has a tree, Christmas all by himself doesn't sound too great. You know Amaryllis and Stellen would love to have him at our place."

I stack my mittened hand on top of my father's and my heart swells with love. "Thanks. That's a much better idea. And trust me when I tell you, Grams will be thrilled we didn't get a tree!"

My dad guffaws so loudly he temporarily loses control of the truck.

I grip the dashboard in terror. "Hey! One dead

body today is enough. Watch where you're going, buddy."

"Sorry. But if memory serves, Isadora is adamant about which tree is displayed for her proper holiday."

I twist my torso toward him, lean my head back, and open my mouth in mock awe. "So you're telling me she was bossy in real life, too?"

We both laugh at that comment.

"Even though I can't see or hear her like you, Mitzy, I can assure you the cold hand of death could not change my mother. If her ghost is anything like her human form, you will display that silver tinsel tree and you'll like it."

Pressing a hand to my unsettled tummy, I try to stifle my laughter. "Stop. My stomach is still upset. But that quote was almost verbatim. She made me dig that thing out of some storage closet and, once I unpacked the atrocity, I asked her if she wanted me to throw it away, and she flew into a ghost rage! I thought she was going to try to possess me!"

Jacob snickers. "So where did you put it up?"

"Nice. I like that you assume I had to put it up. Which I did. Complete with hand-strung garlands of popcorn and cranberry. But I argued to keep it inside the apartment, where it'll have the least exposure."

He grabs the steering wheel with both hands

and his frivolous mood turns somber. "Did she tell you the story?"

"Yeah. She said after her second husband Max was killed in the accident in Europe, and she lost a kidney, she had to turn her life around. I've heard that part before, but not the part about how much money Max had left her. She put herself in rehab, and when she got sober, the first thing she bought with the money from Max was that tree. And celebrating her first sober Christmas—alone—made her swear never to forget what she sacrificed for her sobriety."

Jacob nods. "It's a pretty sobering story—"

My dark humor jumps at the chance to lighten the mood. "No pun intended!"

He shakes his head. "It was accidental. But the story even convinced your grandpa Cal to let her put up the 'ex-husband tree,' as he called it. He was pretty upset about it the first year, but eventually it became part of our family tradition. I know it's nothing to look at, but it has deep meaning for all of us. I'm sure you've heard one or two stories about Isadora's—or I guess I should say Myrtle's—drunken days."

"Why do you think she started going by her second name after she got sober?"

"Honestly, I don't think it had anything to do with sobriety. Myrtle was the name she associated with Odell. They opened the diner together, named it after her, and then things went south. I have a feeling she dropped her first name as a way to erase some of the pain associated with losing him."

"But Grams said they repaired their friendship at the end, when she was sick. She said he was at her bedside every day."

His eyes drift to the rearview mirror. "Sure, at the end. Think about it, honey. If something happened that prevented you from being with Erick, but you had to live in the same town with him your whole life and he never remarried, because he never got over you, wouldn't you try to put any kind of distance between your heart and that memory?"

A hideous chill washes over my whole body. "I don't ever want that to happen, Dad."

He bites his lower lip and nods. "Your grandmother compromised a lot to make Cal happy. She always used to say it was worth it because she got me out of the bargain, but sometimes I wonder . . ."

We ride in silence for a few minutes as we both ponder the mistakes and losses in our lives.

As the city-limit sign comes into view, he taps one of his hands on the steering wheel. "Hey, I interrupted the story about the body. Did Erick know who it was?"

"He did. It's Wayne Olsen's ex-wife, Carol."

My father draws a sharp breath through his

teeth and shakes his head. "I'd say 'ex-wife' is generous. I know she moved out a long time ago, but it's my understanding she never granted him a divorce. She was Canadian and needed the marriage to give her free access across the border."

Something about the way he says free access prickles my psychic senses. "And why exactly would she need that?"

"Oh, you'll hear about Carol Olsen's many questionable ventures soon enough. Her latest endeavor was something called Carol's Canadian Maple, if I'm remembering correctly. She was either an *importer* or an *exporter* of pure Canadian Maple syrup, depending on who you ask."

"Why do you say it with that look on your face? Do you dislike maple syrup?"

He leans back as though I've offended him. "Listen, you don't grow up this far north without a deep, abiding respect for maple syrup. What I dislike are Carol's underhanded practices."

"So you don't think Twiggy killed her?"

Jacob stomps the brakes, and the truck fishtails wildly. He calmly counter steers and gets the vehicle under control at the side of the road, or as close to the side as he can get without driving into the huge snowbank. "Twiggy? Why on earth would Twiggy kill her? Does Erick think she's a suspect?"

"He seemed a little concerned when we first

found the body. I reminded him that Twiggy was at the bookshop when we left, but, as Wayne's girl-friend, I think they'll put her on the suspect list."

My father scoffs darkly. "Speaking from experi-ence, I hope she has a rock-solid alibi."

"Do you think an entitled cat and a sassy ghost can testify in court?"

Chuckles abound as he turns down the al-leyway between our two buildings and pulls into his garage.

"Hey, I'm serious about inviting Erick. He's more than welcome for Christmas Eve supper across the way." Jacob gestures over his shoulder and grins. We continue our walk toward the metal side door of my bookshop and I wrap my arms around his huge barrel chest and squeeze. "Thanks for coming to get me, Dad. I really needed to get out of there. You know?"

He returns the hug and kisses the top of my snow-white head. "The way I see it, I have twenty-plus years of fathering to make up for. You call me for a rescue any time—day or night."

Pulling back, I look up into his eyes and smirk. "You remember who you're talking to, right?"

He laughs and musses my hair as though I'm still a kid. "Yeah, I might be in for more than I bar-gained for, eh?"

"See ya later!" I call out.

He waves as he slips into the side door of the Duncan Restorative Justice Foundation.

I'm eager to race up the wrought-iron circular staircase to share the big news with Grams, but a sense of duty compels me to fill in Twiggy first.

I can barely see the top of her grey pixie cut peeking above the dilapidated rolly chair as she types our weekly order into the vintage computer.

"Twiggy, you got a minute?"

She slowly rotates the chair toward me, her countenance a textbook image of exasperation. "I don't see a tree, kid. Even you can't be that blind. They're all over the place out there."

She kicks the heel of one of her biker-boot-clad feet onto the opposite knee and slaps her hand on her dungarees as she cackles.

Swallowing hard, I tiptoe toward the unsettling news. "Unfortunately, there was also a body up there."

Her normally sarcastic expression melts away, and she leans forward with concern. "Anybody I know?"

"I'm afraid so. Erick said it was Carol Olsen."

Now the color truly drains from her skin, like the fading glow of an old CRT television screen as it powers down. "Carol? Was he sure?"

"I guess. I didn't take that close of a look. Plus, I don't know what she looks like."

"Does Wayne know?"

I cross my arms and hug them around my stomach. "You better hope not."

Twiggy gets to her feet and rakes a hand through her short bangs. "It was murder?"

"Definitely. Shot through the gut. One bullet. Dead center. Too precise to be an accident."

She leans forward, glances both directions, and whispers, "You gettin' any leads? You know, psychic stuff?"

My shoulders shrug involuntarily. "I got the hit about there being a body, but nothing else—yet."

She rubs a hand across her chin and reaches for her cell phone. "I should call Wayne."

Putting my hand on her arm, I shake my head. "I know you want to break it to him gently, but I think it would be better if he shows genuine surprise when Erick gives him the news."

Twiggy slowly lowers her hand and drops the phone on the desk. "Good point." Her eyes snap into focus and she tilts her head back. "Boy, lucky for us you're on the side of the good guys, doll."

"Gee, thanks." Eager to change the subject, I dive into the mundane. "Did you feed Pyewacket this morning, or am I going to get scolded when I walk into the apartment?"

"I haven't seen him. And I sure as sunshine didn't feed him, but who's to say what Isadora might've done." She angles her body away from me, but I can still see the smirk on her sarcastic little face as she pokes fun at my complete lack of control over my ghost roommate's activities.

I check the floor for any evidence of a bowl, and shrug. "I suppose I'll head up there and take what's coming to me."

She sighs and returns to her duties. "Everyone thinks I work for you at the Bell, Book & Candle, but, truth be told, we all work for his royal furriness!"

"Ain't that the truth!" I call out in solidarity.

Carefully stepping over the "No Admittance" chain at the bottom of the spiral staircase, I climb the treads and slowly make my way across the Rare Books Loft. The oak reading tables sit in neat rows like model students, and each one holds a brass lamp with a green-glass shade. The scent of mystery and possibility hangs in the air.

The last scholarly "open reading" session was the previous weekend, so we'll have the loft to ourselves until the New Year.

When I first came here, I didn't understand the true value of this collection. Twiggy and I still fight about whether the chain needs to be hooked all the time, but I finally understand what's at stake. More than once someone has stolen a book from this collection, and both times it ended badly. But that's another story.

Right now, I have to face the potential wrath of a spoiled caracal, and get Ghost-ma to help me set up the murder wall.

CHAPTER 3

THE SECRET BOOKCASE door whooshes closed behind me and the apartment appears empty. Isadora could be on the third floor of the adjacent printing museum, working on her memoirs, but I have no idea what's happened to the furry tan terror.

"Grams? Pyewacket?"

Nothing.

The fiendish feline has all kinds of mysterious ways to come and go as he pleases, so his absence is of little concern. However, I strongly suspect that Ghost-ma is still having a pout over our holiday-tree discussion. Luckily, I know the one thing her ghost finds irresistible.

Pushing the large, rolling corkboard into the center of the room, I clear my throat dramatically.

"Oh well, looks like I'll have to set up the murder wall all by myself!"

Twiggy purchased this corkboard for me, and keeps me supplied with tacks, 3 x 5 cards, and green yarn. I'm not allowed to put tacks into the authentic lath and plaster walls, and I'm also not allowed to use red yarn, because it gives my resident ghost the heebie-jeebies.

"Since nobody wants to hear my juicy gossip, I suppose I'll head over to the diner and grab some lunch."

Turning to leave the apartment, I run smack dab into a translucent wall of vintage burgundy Marchesa silk and tulle.

"Did you say gossip? And murder?"

"Like a moth to the flame." I cross my arms and offer a smug grin while she fully materializes. It really does take all the fun out of it when she's so predictable.

"Listen to me, young lady, don't you pretend to know the first thing about me—"

"Hold on!" I wag my finger back and forth at her shimmering form. "We have a rule in this bookshop. If these lips aren't moving, you don't get to comment. No thought-dropping. No exceptions."

She places a bejeweled fist on her hip and rolls her ghostly eyes. "There have been exceptions. Sometimes you're in danger, and the only way we can communicate is telepathically. Or when you're trying to hide things from Erick, or when—"

"All right. Point made. But this wasn't one of those times. Now, do you want to hear my tale or not?"

At the mention of a tale, Pyewacket saunters out of my massive walk-in closet as though he owns the place. He flicks his thick tan tail and twitches his black-tufted ears.

I've nicknamed the home for a seemingly limitless supply of couture the *Sex and the City* meets *Confessions of a Shopaholic* closet, and it's the place where my grandmother made a physical manifestation of her love for me. Before she died, she carefully packed the closet with precious vintage items from her own illustrious collection, as well as a gargantuan supply of updated items she thought I'd need. My tendency to fall back on jeans and snarky T-shirts is a bit of a bone of contention between us.

"Bone of contention!" Isadora arches a perfectly drawn brow.

"Grams! What did we just talk about?"

She clutches one of her strands of pearls and sighs. "I'm sorry, dear. That was an honest mistake. I'm telling you, it's all jumbled together for me. I'm never sure if you've said it out loud or just thought it."

Taking a deep breath, I point a finger toward

my lips, but before I can chant the mantra, she steals my thunder.

"I know, I know. If those lips aren't moving, blah blah blah." She swirls toward the coffee table, snatches up the pen, and floats it above the stack of 3 x 5 cards. "Let's get on with this murder investigation, shall we?"

I peel off my winter layers and collapse onto the overstuffed settee. "We shall." Quickly bringing her up to speed on the corpse in the forest, I offer the short list of potential suspects.

Her ethereal head is shaking firmly before I finish the list. "Twiggy? Do you really want me to make a card for Twiggy? You said yourself, she was here at the bookshop when Erick picked you up for the outing."

"True, but we don't have time of death yet. She could've been out at the cabin early this morning and made it back to town, before Erick picked me up."

"Reeeee-ow." A warning from the caracal.

"Pshaw! You can't possibly believe that."

The tag-team of opposition irks me, and I stubbornly cross my arms. "Look, one thing I've learned since these psychic powers clicked on is that everyone's a suspect until they're not. So make a card for Twiggy, or I'll get a new assistant."

Right on cue, Pye jumps onto the coffee table

and pushes the stack of 3 x 5 cards onto the floor with his large paw.

Grams and I both crack up.

"Sorry, dear. I didn't mean to lose my temper. Twiggy's been my best friend for more years than either of us would like to count, and I absolutely know in my heart of hearts that she could never kill someone."

"Copy that. But since you don't actually have a heart, we're going to make a card for her and see where it takes us. To be fair, I don't think she's guilty, but I also wouldn't want to be on the wrong side of an argument with her, if you know what I mean?"

Grams giggles. "Oh Mitzy, you're too much."

Approaching the vast empty corkboard, I tack a card for Twiggy, one for Wayne, and, in the center, a card for our victim—Carol. The green yarn connects them all and that's not a good thing.

As I stare at the unhelpful index cards and tap my finger on my chapped lips, the face of my lawyer and alchemical mentor pops into my head. "Oh brother! I was supposed to meet Silas for an early lunch at the diner!"

Running into the closet, I wiggle out of my tree-cutting outfit and shout for my otherworldly stylist. "I'm supposed to go to some kind of solstice thing at his house. What do I wear to a solstice thing?"

Grams phases through the wall, flickering with excitement. "Is he having the full coven?"

"The what now?"

"Well, back when I was a practicing witch, Silas used to host the winter solstice celebration every year for our coven."

"Spoiler alert, I'm not a witch, Grams. And I'm also not in the coven." Lowering myself to the padded mahogany bench in the middle of fashion central, I wait for further details.

"Oh, I know, honey. But with your psychic gifts, and the transmutations Silas has taught you, you've got more talent in your pinky finger than most of those old biddies."

I wiggle my left hand toward her, brandishing my mood ring. "I think you mean in my ring finger."

She giggles, whooshes through me, and dives into the clothes. "You'll need something warm, for the part where you go outside to light the Yule Log — Unless he's doing that inside this year? It also needs to say celebration, with a hint of winter and . . ."

Yawning loudly, I glance at an imaginary watch. "Is this outfit gonna materialize anytime soon, Isadora?"

"I'll have three, or maybe two, options in about ten minutes. You better text Silas that you'll be running late for lunch. And whatever you do, don't go into that cave!"

"Pretty sure there's not a cave at the diner." Maybe she's going ghost crazy.

"I'm not— Never mind. I'm talking about that cave in the cliffs out at Silas's mansion. You told me you went down and explored it? Am I misremembering?"

She's right. I know exactly which cliffs she's talking about now. "No way! That cave is located down a treacherous set of steps that aren't easy to climb in the summer. I certainly won't be following him down that death slide in the winter. After all, what would be the point?"

Grams presses her hands to her chest and sighs with melancholy. "Silas takes his solar holidays very seriously. The entire coven used to build a large bonfire in the cave and sleep there overnight, keeping the fire burning brightly as we each took our shift urging the sun to be reborn on solstice morning. Earth-based traditions believe in honoring nature's cycles. Planting cycles, solar cycles, lunar cycles . . . You get the idea."

I really didn't get the idea, but I understood the concept of sleeping in a cold cave in the middle of winter, and I knew for certain I wouldn't be doing it. "Well, let's hope that item has been removed from the ceremonial agenda. It sounds awful."

Ghost-ma suddenly ceases her rifling through the clothes and drifts toward the well-lit ceiling. "I'm not describing it right. It was truly magical. A group of women, feasting and celebrating together, is heartwarming. The night-long vigil brought us all together. We had to rely on the person keeping watch to build up the fire and keep us all warm. Emerging from the cave at sunrise and feeling like our modest effort somehow insured the new dawn — It's indescribable."

The emotion in her voice almost makes me reconsider my stance on cave camping, but not entirely. "It sounds lovely, Grams. I'm going to try to do something with my hair, and throw on a little makeup. Which should make you happy. When I get back, there better be an outfit waiting."

She claps her hands together with glee at the mention of makeup. "Don't you worry. I will not disappoint you, sweetie."

Splashing warm water on my face in the bathroom, I can hear the hangers sliding back and forth in the closet. It's actually a little eerie to know that I'm technically alone in the apartment, and yet there's something in my closet. One of the many conundrums of living with an earthbound spirit.

Makeup has never come easy with me, and whenever I get stressed about which things to apply in which order, or feel like giving up altogether, I think back to the precious moments I was able to spend with my mother before she was taken from me too soon.

Memories of sitting on various counters in the bathrooms of the different places we called home, watching her "put on her face," wash over me. With my developing psychic skills, I'm able to replay the memory in more detail. I can hear her comforting voice explain each step to me as though she were sitting beside me.

"This is called foundation, and it covers up any imperfections so I look ready to conquer the world."

The sound of her voice echoing through time makes me feel invincible.

"The blush gives my cheeks a little color so no one can tell I'm running on four hours' sleep."

I had forgotten how hard she worked to keep a roof over our heads. Time erases so much.

"This cinnamon mocha lip tint gives me a confident smile, but keeps it professional."

My lips are the picture of hers. My smile is a link to her love.

"A gentle application of smoky shadow gives my eyes depth and intelligence. Not that I'm not intelligent; this just confirms their suspicions."

I may share my eye color with my dad, but I know I get my smarts from my brilliant mother.

"Always give the eyebrows a light nudge with a pencil, so you look like you mean business."

Then she would apply a little mascara to my lashes before she coated her own and say, "Dark lashes give you a finished look. Serious but mysterious." And she would kiss the tip of my nose, every single morning until—

As I twist the mascara wand back into the tube, I have to blink back the tears welling up in my eyes.

"I wish I could've known your mother, Mitzy." Grams' face pushes through the wall from the closet, and glistening ghost-tears trickle down her cheeks.

"Me too. Maybe next year Silas will teach me how to run a proper séance and we can both talk to her." Our eyes meet in the mirror and she nods before slipping back to her wardrobe duties.

"I'll be there in a minute. Just need to do some hair zhuzhing." My skill with the styling wand has improved at least a thousand percent since my arrival in almost-Canada. I never would've expected a ghost to be the one to teach me the ropes, but, truth be told, Grams is rather amazing.

My eyes shimmer with unshed tears and I touch the dream catcher necklace around my neck as I whisper to my mother. "I love you, Mama. I'll never forget you. Thank you for being my mom, even if it was only for a short time. You gave me everything I needed to survive. I wish you could see me now."

Blast it! A couple of those unshed little buggers manage to trickle down my freshly blushed cheeks. Grabbing a tissue, I carefully dab at the moisture on my face and head to the closet to take my medicine.

"Well, what are we looking at? Is there any way I can avoid a four-inch heel in this weather?"

Ghost-ma ignores my taunt and gestures with her arm in a wide arc toward the two outfits she's selected.

One involves an extravagant wrap-around cape that I can't even begin to understand how to deploy, and the other seems a good compromise. Lovely black slacks with enough stretch to be comfortable for a feast, and a soft red sweater, with an appropriate neckline.

"I'm sure you already guessed, but I'm choosing the sweater."

"It's fine. It's the time of year for generosity, so I'll let it slide. I even selected a smart shearling-lined boot with barely a two-inch heel!"

I fan myself as I pretend to faint. "Oh, my stars! The little Christmas elves are smiling down on me."

Grams giggles. "Don't you mean smiling *up* at you?"

"Good one. I set you up for it, but still—"

She whirls around the closet grabbing jewelry

and other accessories, while I suit up for my lunch and the evening's solstice party.

"Am I supposed to take anything? Like a host gift or something for the ceremony?"

She stops so suddenly she appears as a single frozen frame from an old-fashioned cartoon reel. But before the heat of the bulb can bubble the cellulose, the film picks up speed. "You're supposed to take two things. You need to have something that represents a bad habit or memory that you want to release from the past year, and then you need to offer something that represents a positive thing you want to achieve or incorporate in your life in the coming year."

"That sounds kind of complicated. I don't have any ideas, do you?"

Pyewacket struts into the closet, pushes past me with his powerful left shoulder, and rises on his hind legs to thwack a drawer with his paw.

"Seems like you're trying to tell me something, is that right?"

"Reow." Can confirm.

I step toward the drawer and, as I pull it open, my extra senses pick up the word "gun." "You want me to get rid of my only means of protection, son? Are you crazy?"

"Ree-OW!" A warning punctuated by a threat.

Grams floats toward me and hovers at eye level.

"Maybe you should listen to Mr. Cuddlekins, dear. He has a sixth sense about these things. That gun has definitely done more harm than good. You have so many other skills. Skills that only you can wield. Just think about it."

Far be it from me to question this ghost/cat onslaught any further. Reaching into the back of the drawer, I pull out the firearm and slip it into the red-and-grey velvet evening bag I've been instructed to carry. "I'll see what Silas has to say. Now what's the 'good thing'?"

Both Grams and I look at Pyewacket to see if the wise feline has any additional information. He picks that exact moment to rock back on his haunches and take care of some personal hygiene.

Just when you think you're in the presence of true genius!

Grams laughs so hard she snorts.

"You're no help at all." When I'm tempted to give up on the "good thing," inspiration strikes. "I know! I'm going to print out one of the pictures of Erick and me from my phone. That's something I could use more of in the coming year."

Grams lifts her glimmering fist into the air and cheers. "Hear! Hear! Bright solstice blessings to that!" Under her breath, she mumbles, "About time."

"Hey, don't judge me because I want to get it

right the first time. Not all of us are interested in having a laundry list of ex-husbands, Myrtle Isadora Johnson Linder Duncan Willamet Rogers."

"Touché." She taps a perfectly manicured finger on her pursed coral lips while I print out the best pic.

Erick was holding my phone high in the air, and my head was snuggled against his broad chest as we both smiled with genuine joy. I think we took that one out on Fish Hawk Island, right before—

My phone rings, and I glance down in horror. "I forgot to text Silas!"

Grams shakes her head and offers a tsk tsk.

Answering the call on the second ring, I slap on my very best manners. "Good afternoon, Mr. Willoughby. Please allow me to apologize for my tardiness. Isadora took an extra long time selecting my outfit. But I'm all set and I have my items for the ceremony. I'll be at the diner in three minutes or less."

CHAPTER 4

CUT TO—

Myrtle's Diner is bustling with holiday activity. Tally has outdone herself with the beautiful home-spun decorations. I have no idea where she finds the time to crochet after a long day on her feet, but her elves and snowmen are stellar. There are even tinsel garlands tacked to the walls and some beautiful holiday-themed vinyl decals on the black-and-white checkered floor. That modern addition has to be the brainchild of Tally's hard-working daughter, Tatum.

I see a familiar face at the counter and wave happily at Quincy Knudsen, former star photographer of the one and only local newspaper. Quince, as his friends call him, was the first recipient of the newly established journalism scholarship at the local high school, and he has helped me on more than one case. But I don't have time for those stories.

Pointing frantically to the corner booth, I shiver with mock worry. Quince takes one look at Silas, widens his eyes, and nods. He's a man of few words on most days, so I'd say that was a bang-up conversation.

As I slide into the booth, I offer an additional series of apologies.

Silas uncharacteristically waves away my concern, and a smile lifts his sagging jowls.

Boy, this holiday spirit thing must be contagious. "Did you already order?"

This question brings back the familiar look of consternation. His bushy eyebrows squeeze together, and he harrumphs as he adjusts his ever-present fusty tweed coat and unusually patterned bowtie. "Such a question must indicate a severe lack of focus. What troubles you?"

Bonus points to the lawyer/secret alchemist. "Erick and I discovered a body this morning when we were supposed to be out cutting Christmas trees."

Surprisingly, this revelation results in a large belly laugh from my mentor, rather than the expected somber nod. He presses his hands on his round paunch, and his jolly cheeks jiggle until they're bright red. He leans forward to brace himself on the table, and the top of his bald head shines like the star on O *Tannenbaum*.

"I'm not sure what I said to give you such a fit of giggles, Mr. Willoughby."

He leans back and takes a deep breath, but before he can launch into a reply, which most certainly mentions my tendency to attract disaster—

The owner, my surrogate grandfather Odell, approaches the table. "Good afternoon, Mitzy. I heard you got yourself into a little trouble this morning."

As usual, news of my exploits has catapulted through the person-to-person wireless in Pin Cherry Harbor. "If you're referring to the incident near Twiggy's cabin, I'll have you know that the sheriff was also present. And I didn't get *myself* into any trouble. I happened to stumble upon the trouble someone else left."

This defensive argument causes another round of laughter from both lawyer and stand-in grandpa.

Odell slides a beautifully cooked cheeseburger and golden-brown french fries in front of me, and a sensible chicken salad sandwich with a house side salad in front of my lunch date.

"Thanks. This looks delicious." I carefully place a napkin in my lap and grab a few extra from the dispenser at the end of the table next to the carefully stacked jams and the salt and pepper.

Silas nods his approval. "You'd do well to protect that sweater. I'd hate for you to suffer the wrath of—"

"Tanya? At the dry cleaner? She can be a real stickler for stains." I lift an eyebrow and stare at Silas in shock. How is it that he was about to mention the ghost of my dearly departed grandmother in front of one of her ex-husbands? It's not like him to make such an amateur mistake. That's my territory.

Silas folds his hands in his lap and nods. "Indeed. She's never forgiven me for the damage I did to this shirt."

Odell and I glance at the mystery stain on the off-white shirt, but neither of us dare to ask. The cook is more interested in my holiday plans. "You and the sheriff have big plans for Christmas?"

"Not exactly. His mom is visiting her sister in Florida, as I'm sure you already know, so I think I'm going to invite him to my dad's. What do you think?"

Odell's coffee-brown eyes glisten with emotion, and he rakes a hand through his all-business grey buzz cut. "It's good to be around family this time of year. Makes you appreciate what's important." Before either Silas or I can respond, he raps his knuckles on the silver-flecked white Formica table and returns to his duties behind the grill.

"Perhaps you should invite Mr. Johnson to your celebration, Mizithra."

Uh oh. Formal name territory. Now I know Silas means business. "I'll check with Amaryllis. She seems to enjoy entertaining, so I'm sure it won't be a problem. Do you think he'd want to hang out with us?"

Silas steeples his fingers and carefully bounces his thick chin on the tip of his pointers.

I've come to recognize this signal as a brewing lesson about to be served. Something that I've said or done has triggered his need to create a teachable moment out of my mistake. If I'm going to get a lecture, I may as well hear it with something delicious in my belly. I snatch up a handful of golden-fried potato perfection and shove it in my mouth.

His milky-blue eyes seem to bore through my forehead directly into my grey matter.

"All right. I hear what you're not saying. If I focus and use my gifts appropriately, I'll be able to sense whether Odell made his comment because he was feeling lonely or whether it's just something he likes to say to all his patrons during the holiday season."

I take a long sip of my soda, or, as they call it up north, pop, and swallow. "Here goes." I press my hands against the soft wool on my thighs, close my eyes, and replay the recent conversation with Odell. As I relax and let my extrasensory perception fill in the details, my chest squeezes tight with emotion.

"He's terribly lonely, Silas. He throws himself into his work to try to forget, but he's thinking about Isadora—Myrtle—more often than he's not thinking about her. It breaks my heart."

Silas lowers his interlocked fingers and nods once. "Loss affects us all quite differently. For some, their attachments are many and fleeting. When someone leaves their life for whatever reason, they take a deep breath and move on. Hardly missing a beat. For others, the connections are few and deep. For those individuals, each loss seems to steal a sliver of their soul. A finite resource, which cannot be replaced. As the losses stack up, the soul diminishes. I truly feel that for these rare folks, death is not a result of illness, age, or any other tangible factor. At some point, they simply run out of slices, and at that point they leave us."

I'm not sure why I bothered to put on makeup, since everyone is bringing me to tears and inevitably ruining my hard work. Grabbing another napkin from the dispenser, I dab at my cheeks and wipe carefully under each eye. "Odell's one of the people with the soul connections, right?"

Silas glances through the red-Formica-trimmed

orders-up window and watches the man who makes every plate with love. "He is. And I fear he gave more than one sliver to your grandmother. I don't have your gifts, but I've always sensed a piece of him is hollow. I am certain that would be precisely where your grandmother used to interlock."

Desperate to avoid the intense feels, I grasp at anything to change the subject. "Either tell me about the ceremony or ask me about the dead body."

Silas harrumphs, but nods in understanding. "You may proceed first. What did you discover in the deep, dark woods?"

As I look up to speak, the images of the morning replay in rapid succession. My throat feels dry. Taking another sip of my beverage, I swallow and tell my tale. "So, did you know Carol Olsen? When she was married to Wayne, or maybe after?"

He sighs and gazes into the distance. "I believe I met her once at a function your grandmother held. However, I know little of her, other than the standard rumors that drift about a town like this."

"Erick said she and Wayne were divorced, but my dad said that wasn't the case. He said Carol wouldn't give Wayne a divorce, because she needed free access across the border."

Silas smooths his mustache with a thumb and forefinger. "That may be. As I said, I know little about her. Perhaps I am more familiar with Wayne, socially, at least. He strikes me as an honest man struggling under the burden of doing the right thing."

"Which is?"

"Well, he's always been quite interested in our dear Twiggy. However, unable to move things to the next level with her, they frequently part ways before things can become too entangled."

Leaning toward him, I lower my voice. "I hate to ask this. Do you think—?"

His hunched shoulders seem to unfold before my eyes, and the doddering old man that once sat across from me in our booth now embodies the mighty alchemist lurking within. "I think no such thing. And neither should you."

"Copy that."

His voice is quiet, yet carries immense power. There's no room for argument.

Here's me officially taking Twiggy off my suspect list, whether or not Erick likes it.

CHAPTER 5

ONCE INSIDE THE mothball-scented 1908 Model T, Silas offers me several horsehair blankets. "I recall you being a touch sensitive to the cold. These should do nicely."

If by *nicely* he means scratch like a bag of stinging nettle, then yes. They're fantastic.

We make stops at the dry cleaner, the Piggly Wiggly, and the post office as Silas completes his weekly errands and prepares for a houseguest. Me. At long last, we head out of town toward his remote estate.

As we curve down the meandering drive leading to Mr. Willoughby's brooding mansion, I feel as though I may have literally driven back in time. The narrow private road leading to Silas's home winds through a beautiful birch forest; trees wrapped in black-and-white bark as far as the eye can see.

When the dwelling in the forest looms into view, its perfect eccentricity still enchants me. An awe-inspiring Gothic structure, with three haunting stories and small dormers in the roof, which indicate a possibly usable attic space. Sharply pointed turrets accent the corners, and intricate stained-glass windows catch the late afternoon sun. The home is not in disrepair, but it has clearly waged a lengthy battle with time and has given up a little ground with each passing year. A grey stone wall, higher than my head, encloses the property.

On my first visit, I entered through the black iron gate, bearing a faintly familiar sigil, which aligns with the once-grand front entrance of the home. Today we venture down another route.

Silas takes a hidden turn to our right and slips around behind the hulking home, pulls into the garage that was once a carriage house, and leads me through the servants' entrance.

"Even though we didn't come through the impressive front door, this place still reminds me of a fairytale castle."

"One doesn't think of one's home in those terms. I simply enjoy the isolation this location provides." He shuffles toward the kitchen. "I shall put the kettle on and bring you a nice hot chocolate in the drawing room."

I'd love to point out that most simple homes don't have chandeliers and drawing rooms, but my teeth are chattering so hard I'm worried I might bite off my own tongue if I attempt to form more words. Rubbing my arms furiously, I search for any indication of warmth.

"You'll come upon a rich bed of coals glowing in the hearth. Feed them some strips of birchbark and layer the split wood on the resulting flames. You shall find yourself as toasty as a marshmallow in moments."

Doubtful, but the promise of fire brings me hope. When I see the glowing pile of embers, I have to stop myself from jumping into the fireplace.

With shaky hands, I perch on the split-rock hearth and follow his instructions. The papery birchbark feels like a cross between leather and tissue paper. If I weren't so cold, I'd spend more time admiring it and less time tossing it into the fire.

A hearty crackle and the aroma of burning wood reward my efforts. Slowly heat seeps into my bones, and my shivering shoulders relax.

The view in the solstice-eve light is breathtaking. The mansion sits atop a bluff overlooking the great lake, frozen in the grip of winter's icy hand and painted pinkish-gold. For a moment it's as though I've been transported to the Arctic Circle.

By the time Silas joins me, flames are roaring, and I've had to slip back to a footstool. I'm starting to feel my fingers and toes again.

He offers me the cocoa, and I gratefully slurp down the warm liquid. The alcoholic afterburn surprises me. "Whoa! You forgot to mention it was fully *leaded* cocoa."

He chuckles and wipes some whipped cream from his mustache as he lowers himself into an ancient leather recliner. "It's a celebration."

His mention of festivities reminds me. "Grams asked if the entire coven would be here. Will they?"

Silas draws a deep, slow breath and presses his tonsured head against a worn spot on the chair. "Ah, yes. The coven. I fear that once your grandmother passed, I broke ties with the remaining women."

"What happened? Did you lose interest?"

He harrumphs and smooths his bushy mustache with thumb and forefinger. "Truth be told, I never had much interest. My involvement primarily revolved around assisting your grandmother to expand her knowledge and get closer to her true goal."

"Did she want to be high priestess?" A bit of

whipped cream sticks to my lip and I lick it off with a satisfied hum.

He sighs and shakes his head. "Have you learned nothing since you arrived?"

My cheeks flush and I move closer to the fire to hide my embarrassment. "Oh, right. You mean her goal of staying on this side of the veil."

"Indeed. It was a complicated stratagem that required a certain level of expertise on both parts. Your grandmother did a great deal of work to gain the opportunity to meet you, Mizithra."

Holding my hands around the warm mug, I turn toward Silas. "I'm not sure I can ever express how truly grateful I am for the gift that she gave me, and the help that you gave her. Growing up without a family left a hole in my heart. I guess I didn't realize how big that hole was until I arrived here and filled it with Ghost-ma, Jacob, Pyewacket—"

Silas chuckles and sips his hot chocolate.

"And you! Present company included."

He waves off my delayed addition. "I have no concern for my name being listed, my dear. I had someone else in mind."

The heat on my cheeks is definitely cherry-red now. "Oh, you mean Erick?"

He smiles with satisfaction. "The two of you

make a lovely team. I'm glad you chose to remain with us. The town, and indeed I, are better for it."

I set my empty mug on the hearth and wring my hands as I ask my pressing question. "If it's just you and me, do we have to sleep in the cave?"

Unfortunately, Silas has taken a sip of his cocoa, but he's forced to spit it into his thinning handkerchief, as he's unable to stifle the guffaw my question prompts.

"What? Grams is the one who couldn't stop talking about the cave! How do I know?"

He wipes his mouth and gets to his feet. "I must get this kerchief into some cold water immediately. Good chocolate can leave a dastardly stain."

As he shuffles toward the kitchen, I call out, "You didn't answer my question."

He pauses and replies without turning. "We shall enjoy a lovely feast for two, and you and I will light the Yule Log in the library fireplace. There will be no sleeping in caves, my dear."

My anxious shoulders drop as I exhale, and he's still chuckling under his breath all the way to the sink.

A surprisingly cheerful voice beckons me. "Mizithra, can you lend a hand?"

When I enter the kitchen, he's pulling a succulent ham from the oven, and the aroma brings an audible growl from my stomach. "That looks delicious."

He nods proudly and gestures toward the casserole dish still inside. "Select a potholder, and follow me to the dining room."

Sixteen chairs surround the massive cherrywood table spanning the formal dining room. Three candelabras grace the red tablecloth, and between each is an array of poinsettias, pine boughs, and red-beribboned bundles of mistletoe.

For a moment I wonder if we'll be playing out a scene from *Beauty and the Beast*, with me sitting at one end of the ridiculously long table, and Silas at the other, but I see the two places are laid across from each other on the left.

The silverware is polished to a glistening sheen, and gold chargers are each layered with a plate and delicately folded gold napkin. There are two pieces of etched crystal above the plate, a water glass and a champagne coupe.

"Wow! What a beautiful place setting. Is there anything else I need to grab from the kitchen?"

"I shall retrieve the bread, and we will discuss the meaning of solstice while the meat rests."

Leave it to Silas to invent a way to delay gratification even further. Placing the casserole dish on a marble trivet next to the ham, I take my seat and fill my glass with water.

Suddenly overcome with a fit of manners, I hop up and fill his water glass too. I don't see any open wine or champagne, and even I know it would be rude to poke around.

As I return to my seat, Silas enters bearing a beautiful crusty loaf of bread that has been scored to look like an actual log.

"That's so cool. Did you do that?"

He shakes his head and places the bread on the table. "While I am more than capable of making bread, the credit for this well-designed loaf goes to cook. She enjoys putting special touches on the holiday menus."

Silas retrieves a large leather-bound book from a side table, takes his seat, and carefully thumbs through the pages until he finds what he's looking for.

I inhale and open my mouth, but Mr. Willoughby's stern look silences my snoopy nature.

"Our forebears relied on the seasons to guide them. A late frost could kill delicate buds on life-giving fruit trees, a pestilence during the growing season could decimate crops, and disease in the livestock could mean death for hungry villagers. In this modern age, we are fortunate to have plenty, but that false sense of security separates us from the important cycles of nature." He turns a thin sheet and runs his finger down the page.

I know better than to open my mouth.

"Winter solstice is a time to celebrate the return of the sun. For each day after this will bring more hours of sunlight, culminating at the summer solstice.

"Our meal this evening consists of cured meats, root vegetables, and our all-important grains. The bounty of the harvests is behind us, and more hard months of winter lie ahead. The sun will grow in strength, and next year our crops will surely prosper. Let us eat this feast with gratitude and remember the precious gift of each day."

Nodding my head, I swallow my emotion. Working at my minimum wage barista job back in Arizona, when I couldn't even pay my bills, life didn't seem very precious. But if I'd given up then, I never would've had this amazing experience in almost-Canada. "Every day is precious, Silas. Thank you for reminding me."

He turns and pulls a bottle of champagne from a bucket of ice that I swear to you did not exist a moment ago. In a flash, he takes the carving knife from the ham platter, and, with one swift motion, slices the cork into the air as he intones, "Bright solstice blessings!"

Silas pours the bubbly into our glasses, clinks his coupe to mine, and, for the first time I can remember, downs his entire serving of champagne in one unceremonious gulp.

"Cheers to that!" I add before following his lead.

He rises and serves the honeyed ham and some glorious dish he calls dauphinoise potatoes.

After two servings of potatoes, a healthy slab of ham, and an overly buttered slice of thick, warm bread, I'm worried I won't be able to move. The stretch in these wool pants is barely getting me by.

"We shall take our wassail in the library. Come with me."

After briefly returning to the kitchen to ladle up two steaming mugs of spiced wassail, he leads the way to the library.

The polished marble floor boasts an impressive collection of rugs. A sturdy oak-legged table in the center is being tested to its limits with the massive selection of tomes lying open on its surface. The arcane collection in this room surely rivals the Rare Books Loft.

Silas guides me to a vintage wing-back chair with tufted sage-green upholstery and dark cherry-wood framing.

Once I'm seated next to the roaring fire, he snaps his fingers, and the room falls into inky darkness. "Silas? Is that supposed to happen?"

"The light of the sun is a powerful resource. Yet, somehow we never miss the light until it is gone."

Oh, this must be part of the ceremony. Probably best if I keep quiet and don't move.

Some rustling in the fireplace confirms my suspicions. Having worked with torn pieces of birchbark earlier, I recognize the distinct papery crinkle. Some twigs are snapped, some logs are stacked, and the alchemist takes a seat in the matching chair next to mine.

"When the light returns, all will be made well." He claps his hands together, and sparks sizzle from the fireplace.

Silver, blue, green, purple, and red flickers of light dance over the pile of logs like miniature fairies.

"Welcome, returning sun. We are grateful for your light, your warmth, and the life you share."

The logs burst into flame, and I watch as the beautifully decorated limb of oak sitting atop the pyre slowly feeds its ribbons, pinecones, and cranberries to the flame.

Silas reaches a hand out in the firelight and pats my arm. "I understand Robin Pyewacket Goodfellow's concern regarding your firearm. However, the solstice flames are not a place to dispose of such an item. You are a complicated woman, with an impressive and expanding skillset in the psychic and alchemical realms. I should leave it to your judgment whether that item remains with you or finds its way to some other. In contrast, I believe the item you wish to place in the bonfire which represents your hopes for the coming year is more appropriate."

I won't even ask how he knows what he knows. He claims he possesses no psychic powers, but as I sit across the marble-topped walnut side table, I think I'm starting to understand why Erick uses the word uncanny so often. I reach into my purse and pull out the photograph.

Silas smiles and nods.

Moving toward the crackling flames, my heart swells with hope. I want to share more with Erick in the coming year. I'm glad we're taking things slow, but I want to pick up the pace—a little. Here's to the coming year, Erick Harper.

With a light kiss, I toss the photo into the fire and feel a tingle of warmth circle my spine.

Glancing toward Silas, I'm about to ask after the next phase of the ritual, but his eyes are closed, and there's a light snoring ruffling his mustache and wiggling his jowls.

Maybe that was enough. Maybe simply being

in the here and now is what I've been missing all these years.

Tomorrow I'll be back on the case, working with Sheriff Too-Hot-To-Handle to keep my cantankerous employee's boyfriend out of jail. But tonight, I can stare into the flames, rub my full belly, and be happy.

CHAPTER 6

MORNING at the mansion is eerily quiet. I walk toward the heavily draped window to see if my efforts have recharged the sun. As I slide the thick brocade to the side, a magical scene unfolds.

Thick flakes of snow are fluttering downward like tiny angels bringing messages to earth. Beyond the sleeping terraced gardens, a large buck feasts on an offering of grains and vegetables that Silas must've placed in the yard before the sun came up.

Hastily dressing in yesterday's wardrobe, I descend the wide staircase as the welcome aroma of coffee wafts upward and envelops me.

"The coffee smells delicious, Silas."

When I enter the kitchen, he pours me a mug and slides a porcelain, cow-shaped creamer toward me. "Will you be joining me for breakfast?"

"Erick asked me to meet him at the diner, but—"

"Certainly. I will be but a moment, then I can ferry you into town."

The last thing in the world I want right now is another subzero ride in his ridiculous excuse for a car. "That's super nice of you, but Erick said he would pick me up. Should I tell him to come around to the back?"

A mischievous grin curls the corners of the alchemist's mouth.

"What's so funny?"

"He will be unable to see the turn, my dear."

"What? Why not? I mean, I know it's kind of on a blind curve, but it's not that hard to see."

Silas strokes his mustache twice and refills his mug. "You can see the turn, because you possess a rare set of gifts. You are but one of three, only two living, who can detect the turn."

"Did you use magic—sorry, alchemy—to hide it? Could Grams see it?"

"Yes, to both. Perception is not fixed. Our eyes can play tricks on us. Using those tricks to create a camouflage is simpler than it sounds. Your grandmother could not always see the turn, but she reached a point in her studies—"

A sudden crack in his voice catches me off guard, and I set my coffee cup on the counter and move to his side. "What is it? What were you going to say?"

"I am certain your grandmother has told you how her relentless pursuit of magical knowledge led to her illness."

"She did. Grams said the doctors chalked it up to liver failure and her early abuses of alcohol. She always believed that delving too deeply into the magical arts ultimately sealed her fate. I don't think there's any way to prove that."

A flash of guilt darts across his wizened face. "There are ways. I know the ways, but instead of discouraging her and putting her health first—"

"What are you saying? You're not responsible for her obsessions. It's very common for addicts to replace one addiction with another. Maybe Alcoholics Anonymous helped her get sober, but they couldn't keep her from magic."

A light of hope flickers in his eyes, and he grips my hand with both of his. A warm, grateful energy floats up my arm. "Thank you, Mizithra. I never truly forgave myself for encouraging your grandmother's wish to tether her spirit. A great burden of responsibility for her choices weighed on me. I could've dissuaded her. For that matter, I could've concealed certain facts, perhaps even convinced her the dream was impossible. A small part of me, certainly vanity, wanted to test the boundaries between dimensions. Your kind words have given me some relief, and, in the end, I helped her achieve something wonderful."

I place an arm around his shoulder and squeeze. "And you gave me an unbelievable opportunity. Getting to know Isadora has changed my life in ways I can't even explain."

Before things can get any mushier, my phone pings with a text.

"Here. Gate locked."

"Erick's here. I know you're not big on crowds, but you're more than welcome to come to my dad's place for Christmas Eve supper."

"I shall consider the invitation. It is most kind."

Grabbing my jacket and purse, I head toward the marble entrance and its sparkling chandelier. "Can you unlock the gate?"

For a moment, I sense a current of electricity in the air.

"It is done." He announces the transmutation as though he's handed me an everyday paper napkin.

"Solstice blessings, Silas!"

His chuckle follows me out the door and is lost in the lovely snow.

Erick pushes through the gate and trudges toward me. "Do you think I should shovel his walk?"

Sweetness overload. It's not as though I can tell him that an alchemist rarely needs help transmuting snow to water or steam, or whatever Silas does. "I think he has someone for that. Thanks for offering."

Erick scoops an arm around my waist and holds me tighter than necessary.

"That's some grip, Sheriff. Did you miss me?"

"Of course I missed you. I've also seen you fall on your backside in the snow more than once. Let's call it a safety precaution."

As we wind toward the main highway, Erick makes small talk. "I thought I remembered there being a back way into his place, but I must've missed the turn."

Looks like Silas was right about the hidden nature of that alternate entrance. Not that it should surprise me. "Yeah, it's a tricky one. Any news about the case?"

He comically hangs his head and chuckles. "Hold your horses. Why don't you tell me about your Yule solstice first?"

"Hey, I'm no *Ben-Hur*. I'm just a curious gal."

I don't appreciate his mocking gasp.

"Since you asked, I believe it's winter solstice or Yule. I don't think you can cram them all together like supercalifragilisticexpialidocious."

Erick taps his thumb on the steering wheel and sings, "Even though the sound of it—"

"Oh brother. Forget I mentioned it."

"Good food, though?"

Pressing a hand to my belly, I sigh in remembrance. "Always. I would kill for that potato recipe. Dolphin something or other . . . It was creamy potato goodness!"

Chuckling, he offers unsolicited commentary. "You have a real strange relationship with root vegetables, Moon."

"Rude. Not root *vegetables*, plural. I happen to enjoy the potato. Many people admire Earth's most perfect food."

He laughs loudly, then rubs a thumb under his eye. "I'm not sure that's scientifically proven, but they are delicious. Was it dauphinoise potatoes?"

My head turns with the ratcheting lag of an animatronic mannequin. "How's that? Are you a secret chef?"

He grips the steering wheel with both hands and eases back into his seat. "Not even close. Since the macular degeneration prevents my mother from reading her cookbooks, she runs all the cooking shows on television, and attempts to re-create the recipes by paying attention to the ingredients they mention on air, or occasionally through online video supplements. She's made that dish a couple of times, and, under duress, I'd be forced to agree that it was—what's that word you're so fond of using?—divine."

"Wow, you're really sticking it to me today, Sheriff. Did you have an espresso this morning?"

He shakes his head. "Nah, I'm running on empty. Maybe I've got some low-blood-sugar-related snark."

"Yeah. We need to get some food in you, stat."

He grins, and his heavenly-blue eyes sweep toward the passenger seat. As they scan over me, I feel my temperature rising. "Can you turn your heater down?"

He glances at the dash, looks at me funny, and arches his eyebrow. "It's already on low. What's happening over there, Moon? Something got you hot under the collar?"

The tingly flush rising from my tummy reaches my cheeks, and I press my face against the window. "It's probably a combination of this ridiculous sweater and the thick winter coat. Nothing for you to be concerned about."

He smirks in a way that makes my stomach flutter as though it's housing a swarm of butterflies.

Attempting to ignore my dry mouth and difficulty swallowing, I move the conversation toward trees. "So, um, since we didn't get a tree—"

"We can head back out there. The crime scene has been processed, and I'm sure the recent snowfall has erased the rest of the unsightly event. Is that what you were going to say?"

"Not exactly." Let's see if I can come at this greased pig of a conversation from a different angle. "Since your mom's in Florida, I was wondering . . . I mean, it seems like maybe—"

"Geez, Moon. I've never seen you so flustered. Should I pull over? Do you need some fresh air?"

His teasing does the trick. I straighten my spine, gulp down some stale car air, and screw my courage to the sticking place, Lady Macbeth style. "I was wondering if you'd like to come to my dad's for Christmas Eve supper." There. I spit the words out in machine-gun rapid-fire, completing the question before I have the chance to lose my courage.

His eyes sparkle and his jaw muscles flex. "Boy, family dinner, and during a holiday, no less. This sounds quite serious. Are you planning some kind of big reveal?" He chuckles as soon as he finishes the sentence, and it's easy to see that he's amusing himself at my expense.

Well, two can play that game. "I didn't want to spoil the surprise, but, yes."

His strong jaw drops, and he turns toward me as the color drains from his face. "You don't— You're not—"

"Oh, keep your eyes on the road, Sheriff. I'm just messing with you. Tit for tat, they say."

He gasps for air and pats his chest. "Okay, you

win. No more games, please. We've got a good thing going. There's no need to tempt fate."

My throat tightens, but I manage to squeak out a response. "You're not wrong."

He parks the cruiser at his spot in front of the sheriff's station and we walk into the diner to a chorus of Merry Christmases, good mornings, and the standard spatula salute from Odell. The weekend crowd has thinned minutely, but we're still fortunate to find an empty booth.

My favorite waitress, Tally, hustles over with a pot of coffee and two empty mugs. Her tightly wound, flame-red bun bobs as she pours our liquid alert and presses for a gossip update. "Gosh, Sheriff, that Carol Olsen case is a real humdinger. Any leads?"

Erick smiles his work smile, which doesn't quite reach his eyes. "You know I can't discuss an ongoing investigation, Tally. You tell the coffee klatch we're looking into a number of possibilities."

She smiles like the cat that swallowed the canary and hustles off.

"Erick! You know better than to give her any ammunition. By the time she shares that with her cronies, she'll have twisted it into a series of arrests and possibly an anonymous out-of-town stranger."

Sliding his hands around his mug of coffee, he nods. "If she doesn't start the rumor, someone else will. As long as they stay away from the facts, I don't much care about the gossip rolling through town."

So levelheaded and methodical. No wonder it takes him so long to get to the truth. "Now that we've talked about my celebration, it's time for you to ante up. Do you have a time of death?"

"I do."

"And? Does it clear Twiggy?"

"Unfortunately, it does not. And to make matters worse, the shot was too precise to be an accident. The bullet didn't pass through the heart, but it was a highly targeted gutshot, meant to allow the victim to bleed out slowly."

I shiver uncontrollably. "Twiggy would never do something like that. That's diabolical. That's an assassin's move, or someone trying to get information."

He walks his fingers across the table and turns his palm upward. As I lay my hand on his, he rubs his thumb across the back of my fingers. "Would it surprise you to know that I agree? The thing is, Twiggy holds three statewide sharpshooter titles. I can't rule her out until I question her, see if she has an alibi, and, if so, confirm it. But in my heart, I don't believe she could do something like this. We're looking into Carol's maple syrup trafficking, but the sugar makers are a tight-knit group. They're not being forthcoming with information."

"Do you want me to go undercover? I can be a confidential informant."

"Settle down, Moon. I don't want you to do anything of the kind. The maple syrup mafia might sound humorous, but it's a dangerous organization protecting a multi-million-dollar syrup trade."

I pull my hand back and place both in the air like a stickup. "Get out of here! Maple syrup mafia? Multi-million-dollar *maple syrup?*"

He shrugs. "I'm sorry to be the one to tell you, but a barrel of maple syrup is worth twenty to thirty times more than a barrel of crude oil."

"Shut the front door!"

Odell slides our irresistible breakfasts onto the table and nods. "I've seen the price go as high as twenty-three dollars for eight ounces of pure Canadian Amber. Those barrel rollers are no joke. If Carol was messing with them, I wouldn't be near as shocked about what happened to her." He lifts his hand to rap his knuckles, but I reach out and grip his arm.

"Odell, would you like to come to my dad's for Christmas Eve supper?"

His face remains stoic, but where my hand touches his skin, I receive a clairsentient flash. A tightly wound ball of emotion. Heartache, wrapped in longing, nearly strangled by loneliness.

"I'll check my schedule." He turns and slides his wrist from my slack grip. No double tap with the knuckles, no parting wisdom.

He doesn't return to the grill. He must've headed straight out the back door of the kitchen. "I'll be right back."

Erick nods and digs into his pancakes without delay.

Pushing open the kitchen door that leads into the alley beside the diner, I find Odell with a tattered cigarette in the corner of his mouth. The first time I witnessed this, I waited for him to light the thing, but I've since learned that he quit smoking over fifteen years ago. He keeps an old cigarette in the pocket of his faded denim shirt to remind him of his struggle with tobacco, and his mother that passed from lung cancer.

The corners of his eyes are wet with tears.

"Hey, I don't mean to intrude."

He waves a hand in the air and shakes his head. "It's not your fault. It's a tough time of year. I appreciate the invitation, but it's best if I keep to myself. No point in bringing everyone down during the holidays."

"Look, I respect everyone's traditions. Before I came here, I used to spend Christmas watching

FailArmy videos on my phone, and stuffing my face with leftover pizza, or Chinese food. And that was only the years when I had a phone plan that was paid up. Sometimes it was just the pizza and a blank wall."

He looks toward me, and the ache in his eyes is palpable.

I hurried outside without my coat, and the windchill from the great lake nestled in our harbor is starting to work its way through my sweater. "I know I told you this before, but I absolutely think of you as my surrogate grandfather. We would love to have you at the family dinner, but no pressure. Seriously. Think it over. There's always room for you at our table."

He struggles to swallow, can't find the words, and nods sharply.

It doesn't take a psychic to see that the man needs some privacy. Squeezing his shoulder once, I return to the booth to enjoy my scrambled eggs with chorizo, and my dashing breakfast date.

CHAPTER 7

ERICK OFFERS to walk me back to the bookshop, to keep me from any snow- or ice-related disasters. However, as we get nearer to the Bell, Book & Candle, I sense a rising tension in my escort. "Is there something you're not telling me about this door-to-door service, Sheriff?"

Shaking his head, he mutters, "You and your hunches."

"Spare me. Just answer the question." I elbow him playfully in the side.

"I was hoping if I talked to Twiggy in familiar, neutral territory, she'd be more likely to cooperate."

"Thanks a lot."

He pulls his arm close to his side and my arm gets squeezed between his powerful bicep and taut abdomen. "Ah, don't be like that. You know Twiggy is a tough nut to crack. Anything I can do to keep her from getting defensive is in her own best interest."

"Copy that. If you want to stay on her good side, don't accuse her of anything. She's smart enough to know she's a suspect, but if she thinks you're actually considering her, she's likely to lock up tighter than Fort Knox."

"Thanks, Moon. And if I didn't say so earlier, I'd be honored to come to the dinner at Jacob's. Thanks for asking."

My breath catches in my throat. I busy myself with door-opening duties and rush inside before he can say anything more sentimental.

"Twiggy? Twiggy, are you here?"

She leans over the thick balustrade, which curves in a large semi-circle along the edge of the second-floor loft. "Up here, doll. I'm shelving some of the new collection."

Erick and I head up to the Rare Books Loft, and Twiggy walks toward us, with arms firmly crossed and her mouth pinched in a fine line.

My brain flips through possible opening lines, and I keep coming up empty. Thankfully, Erick strides past me and reaches out his hand in a friendly gesture. "I'm sure you know why I'm here, Twiggy. I thought it would be better if we had an informal chat, rather than making things official down at the station."

She taps her toe impatiently and does not take his outstretched hand. "Ask me anything you like, Sheriff. I've got nothing to hide."

"Can you tell me where you were Saturday evening between 8:00 p.m. and midnight?"

"I can." She offers nothing further.

Erick nods politely. "And where were you?"

"I was at home, in my own bed, like all good citizens of Pin Cherry."

"Understood. Can anyone confirm that?"

For the first time, Twiggy's confidence wavers, and she breaks eye contact.

Stepping forward, I offer my two cents. "You're not really a suspect. He just needs your alibi. Isn't there anything you can tell him?"

Her energy shifts suddenly, as though she's had a bolt of inspiration. She glances at Erick, and the corners of her mouth turn up for a split second. "I had a guest. I'm sure he can vouch for me."

For the first time in my life, I sense she might not be offering us a completely forthright answer.

He jots a couple of notes on his pad. "Can you give us this person's name, please?"

Twiggy lifts her chin. "Wayne Olsen."

Erick's pen comes to a halt on the paper, and he

narrows his gaze. "Wayne Olsen spent the night at your house? What time did he arrive?"

She uncrosses her arms and shoves one hand in the pocket of her dungarees. "He came for supper, about 5:30."

"Okay. And what time did he leave?"

She hesitates for a moment and looks up to the right. "He left when I headed to the bookshop. So, that was around 8:30 a.m."

Erick finishes his notes, replaces the notepad and pen in his pocket, and offers a perfunctory smile. "Thank you. I'll be in touch if I have any further questions. I appreciate your cooperation today."

She shrugs. "No problem. I told you, I have nothing to hide." Turning, she grabs a book from her cart and climbs up the large ladder that spans almost two stories of shelving.

Remaining neutral and silent, I follow Erick down to the first floor.

"I'll be heading back to the station. I'll let you know if the medical examiner comes up with any additional details. I know it's pointless to ask, but I really wish you'd stay out of this one, Mitzy."

Oh boy, he's using my first name. This is a serious request. "You know I can't. Twiggy is like family. I have to find out who actually did this."

He leans close, as though he's going to kiss my

cheek, but whispers, "I don't think she's being completely above board with her alibi. But I think you already know that."

I kiss him on the cheek instead, and smile too brightly. "I'll let you know what I find out, Sheriff."

He exhales loudly and heads out of the bookshop.

Staring at Twiggy's back, high above on the ladder, I can easily tell she's in no mood for further conversation. Time to tap my ghostly resource for details of Pin Cherry's past. Grams was a wealthy and influential woman. She knew everyone worth knowing and probably plenty who swam in lower circles, but possessed useful information.

As the bookcase door slides open, Pyewacket leaps off the bed, dragging something in his mouth. When he gets closer, I see it's one of the strands of popcorn and cranberry that hung on the tinsel tree. However, it's obvious he's eaten all the popcorn, and the strand only contains cranberries.

"It's not going to be a very festive Christmas if you eat all the decorations, Pye." I pick up the badly battered strand of garland and turn toward the trash can. Before I can make it a single stride, the familiar thwack of a powerful caracal paw assaults my ankle.

He kindly left his needlelike claws retracted, so I know it's only a warning. "Message received. I will hang on to this disgusting piece of trash and see how it fits into our puzzle at a later date." Holding the gross, slobber-wet thread in one hand, I retrieve a tack and add Pyewacket's *evidence* to the murder board.

CHAPTER 8

AFTER SEVERAL UNSUCCESSFUL attempts at summoning the ghost of Isadora, I'm on the hunt.

It's not as exciting as it sounds. If she's not following me around snooping in my love life or telling me what to wear, she's usually in the adjacent printing museum.

I push through the "Employees Only" door from the bookshop, and the smell of ink, metal, and history hits me as I walk across the polished concrete floor.

The space is only half the size of the bookshop, but it has an entire second floor rather than balconies and a mezzanine. The ground floor houses large equipment and a variety of historical displays, including an authentic Gutenberg press.

Trudging up the steps to the third floor, I pause

and take in the scene.

My new stepbrother, Stellen, is home on winter break from his freshman year in college. Last year when his father was killed, we discovered that Stellen could see ghosts. And in that department, he's actually got me beat. Not only can he see the ghosts of humans, but he can also see animal ghosts. He can't hear Isadora, but he can see her, and when she's got enough energy to pick up a pen and write messages, they have lovely conversations.

Currently, he's looking over her memoirs and explaining the process of scanning her handwritten pages to convert them into editable files through character recognition software.

As you might've guessed, Isadora isn't picking up much of what he's laying down.

"Stellen! I was wondering when I was going to get a chance to see you."

He drops the stack of sheets he's sorting and strides past the antique photo-engraving display to give me a hug.

"I hate to be this big sister, but you've grown like a foot!"

He blushes, and his bright-green eyes avoid mine as he smooths a lock of long, black, wavy hair behind his ear. "It's only like six inches. No big deal."

Giving him another one-armed hug, I press him

for details. "All right, so you grew six inches, your hair also grew six inches, and you're home for two or three weeks. What are you doing hanging out with Ghost-ma? Why aren't you at your girlfriend's?"

He pulls away and chews his bottom lip. "Yolo and I are taking a break."

"What? Why? Did something happen?"

"No. Nothing bad. She's got a really intense schedule at MIT, and I need to finish at the top of my class if I want a scholarship for veterinary school."

Reaching out, I grab his nervous hand and squeeze. "Hey, college is about experiences too, not just grades. And you know there'll always be a Duncan-Moon scholarship for you." I offer him a giant wink, and point foolishly at my eye as I repeat the wink multiple times.

He leans back and attempts a scowl. "Something wrong with your eye, sis? You should get that checked out."

I punch him playfully on the shoulder. "Now there's the little brother I missed." I walk past him, but as I approach the task Grams is working on she opens a drawer and scoops her memoirs into it.

"That's pretty *su-spish*, Isadora. You got something to hide?"

She crosses her arms over her full figure and

shakes her head. "I'm an artist, dear. I don't like people looking at my work until it's finished."

"He's looking at it." I gesture toward Stellen. "Why does he get to look at it, and I don't?" I kick out a hip and plant my fist on it.

"Because he's helping me with technical issues. I need to get the first five chapters to the publisher by mid-January."

Glancing at Stellen, I give him a thumbs-up. "That's great. I'm so happy you found a publisher who's interested in it, Grams. But, I'm family. Don't you think I should get the opportunity to read it before it's published?"

Stellen snickers, but quickly puts a hand over his mouth.

I narrow my gaze and stare each of them down in turn. "I smell a rat. Or some other nefarious creature. You two are in league, and I don't like it."

Grams floats toward me and waves her hand dismissively. "Oh, don't be so dramatic, sweetie. There's nothing for you to be concerned about. I'm only asking for a little privacy while I'm creating."

Crossing my arms, I tilt my head and click my tongue. "Oh, it's privacy you want? Because you're so good at returning the favor, right?"

All three of us crack up at that statement, and Grams lifts her ethereal arms in the air. "Mea culpa. Mea culpa."

Taking a quick breath, I return to the original purpose of my ghost hunt. "I'm actually glad you're both here. I'm in the middle of this case, and it never hurts to get another perspective on new info."

Stellen's eyes brighten. "Is it a ghost?"

"Not yet. But I've learned to never say never with the spirit world. Here's what we know so far—"

I bring them up to speed on the latest in the Carol Olsen case, and then I ask Grams the question that led me to the third floor. "So, I was wondering if you know anyone in the maple syrup trade? Either here, or in Canada, but here would be better. I need to get some more information on what kind of business Carol was running, and if she really was in league with, or poaching from, the maple syrup mafia."

Stellen laughs again. "Sorry, can't help it. It just sounds like some kind of oxymoron. Like the teddy-bear hit squad, or the cuddly-kitten assassins."

Grams and I stare at him with somber expressions.

He gulps and takes a step back.

"Gotcha!" We share a giggle at his expense.

"Well, dear, I was very well connected. However, most of my contacts were the upper echelon of Pin Cherry Harbor society. Can't say I was acquainted with anyone illegally importing Québec's finest."

"What makes you say, Québec?"

Her shimmering eyes widen. "Everyone knows the best maple syrup on the planet comes from Québec."

My eyes dance. "The best maple syrup on the planet?"

Stellen clears his throat. "Arguably."

She zooms toward him, and he puts up his hands in surrender. "Whatever you said is right."

"Easy, Ghost-ma. Don't intimidate my source. Stellen, do you know of some better maple syrup?"

He sidesteps away from the angry ghost and sidles up next to me. "There was a guy who really had a thing for trapping and stuffing skunks. He brought my dad a lot of business when we ran the taxidermy, you know—"

Placing a comforting hand on his shoulder, I nod. "I remember. You don't have to talk about it."

Stellen inhales sharply. "Thanks. So, this guy brought my dad a lot of business, but he rarely paid in cash. We had enough maple syrup to host a pancake breakfast every month for probably five years. But it was, as my dad used to say, 'without peer.'"

"This guy's local? Do you think he's still in the business?"

He scoffs at my lack of experience. "Mitzy,

people don't dabble in maple syrup. It runs in their veins. Once they're in, they're in for life."

My jaw slackens. "It sort of is like the mafia." I lift my chin in an attempt to do a Marlon Brando riff, and growl, "You got a name for me, kid?"

Stellen chuckles at my weak attempt at a Mafioso impression. "Yeah. Ezekiel Elhard."

"Wow, that's a heck of a name. I'm surprised—"

My ringing phone interrupts us, and when I see the name of Silas Willoughby on the screen, I quickly answer. "Good morning, Mr. Willoughby. How may I help—?"

Mr. Willoughby's voice is unusually excited. He doesn't even wait for me to finish my official greeting before he launches into his announcement. I manage to get in one "yes" and two "mmhmms" before he ends the call.

"That was weird."

Grams swirls toward me and places her partially corporeal hand on my shoulder. "You should know better than to say that within these walls, dear."

"Touché. That was Silas. He'd suddenly remembered a local contact that might be able to help us out in the Carol Olsen homicide investigation."

Stellen, Grams, and I all lock eyes. In unison we shout, "Ezekiel Elhard!"

This is the kind of psychic moment that's become everyday grist for the mill in my new life.

"I'm gonna hop in the Jeep and head out to his place as soon as I figure out where that is. You in?" I point to my little brother.

He shrugs. "I don't think I can go. I promised I'd help Isadora today. Amaryllis has a bunch of stuff scheduled this week, so today is really the only day I have to work on this. Um, maybe you should take Erick. Ezekiel is a little out there. Not exactly dangerous, but, you know, out there."

A loud groan escapes. "Fine. I'll text him. But if he's too busy, I'm going by myself. This ain't my first rodeo, son."

Stellen shakes his head. "Nope, not a fan of that expression." He stifles a chuckle and returns to the desk with the ghost of my memoir-obsessed grandmother.

Tromping down the stairs on a return trip to the bookshop, I fire off a text to the sheriff. "I got a lead. Ezekiel Elhard. Change into your civvies. I'll pick you up in five."

There. I've offered him two likely insurmountable obstacles. I'm sure he doesn't have his civilian clothes at work, and I'm positive he won't be able to find a way to free himself from duty in five minutes.

My phone pings, and I look down in satisfaction. The smug grin is instantly wiped off my face as I read, "You're on!"

Blerg.

Changing into skinny jeans, warm boots, and a cable-knit sweater, I stuff mittens into the pocket of my winter coat and tuck it under my arm as I head to the Jeep.

When I pull out of the alley, I encounter a patch of ice. Even though I was a bit of a brat at the time, I'm now grateful that my father insisted on snow tires.

Checking my watch, I'm right on schedule. I figure I'll give Erick thirty seconds leeway and then hit the road on my own.

Unfortunately for me, the fully changed, ready-for-action sheriff is waiting at the curb as I pull up.

He hops onto the passenger seat and the stench of champion wafts throughout my vehicle.

"Fine. You win."

He throws his shoulders back and grins. "Was there ever any doubt, Moon?"

I choose to mumble my response under my breath. "I've created a monster."

He casually glances at his phone, but slips it into his coat pocket. "So, you know the way to Ezekiel's sugar shack?"

Choking on my laughter, I cough to clear my throat. "Did you say sugar shack? Are we in a B52's music video?"

He shakes his head and crosses his arms in that

yummy way that makes his biceps bulge. "You got a lot to learn about the sugar bush industry."

Laughter grips me, and I have to force myself to keep my eyes open and watch the road. "You're just making stuff up now. But, no, I don't know the way to Ezekiel's sugar shack. Why don't you enlighten me, Sheriff?"

Erick becomes my personal GPS and guides me turn by turn to the sugar maker's remote property.

We knock on the front door of the farmhouse, but there's no response. Erick steps off the screened porch and heads toward the woods.

My stomach roils with unwanted memory of the recent corpse in the forest, and I stand my ground.

"You comin'? I know the way to the sugar shack. There was a fire out there a couple years ago."

Oh, what I wouldn't give to have recorded that soundbite. I cannot begin to explain to you how many times I would replay the deep rumbling voice of Erick Harper saying, "I know the way to the sugar shack!" Who needs a winter coat with this kind of heat?

"Coming." Hopping off the last step, I jog toward my own sugar maker. And an embarrassed schoolgirl giggle sucks all the cool straight out of me.

"Come on. It's through this stand of sugar bush."

Glancing at the leafless trees, I shrug. "I'm going to go out on a limb. Is sugar bush another name for maple trees?"

"Pretty much. Technically, it refers to two specific species which are the best for sap production and make the sweetest syrup, particularly trees like sugar maple and silver maple."

"Copy that." As we come to the other side of the leafless brown stand of maple, an ominous building looms into view. The creepy wooden shack could easily be the location of several heart-pounding 80s horror movies. "Yikes. *The Evil Dead* much?"

Erick chuckles. "You only think that because they're not in a production cycle. When you walk through the trees and smell that sap bubbling away, it changes your whole perspective. There's absolutely nothing like a craft stick or hockey stick handle wrapped in fresh Jack wax."

I stop and place one hand on my thigh as I recover from a round of belly laughs. "Seriously, you have to stop. You're killing me."

The door of the sugar shack opens, and a giant of a man strides out with an equally massive rifle—aimed directly at the intruders.

To be clear, we are the intruders.

"You're trespassing, you know. You best hightail it while you have the chance, eh? This blunderbuss ain't for show."

Erick immediately raises his hands in the air, and I follow suit. "Hey, Ezekiel, it's Sheriff Harper. I came in civilian clothes because this isn't an official visit." He gestures toward me. "This here is Mitzy Moon. She's—"

"I'm a friend of Silas Willoughby's. He actually gave me your name. And my stepbrother Stellen Jablonski—his dad used to stuff skunks for you."

Ezekiel lowers the huge firearm and guffaws loudly. "Heck, those are two of my favorite people in the whole world, dontcha know. Come on over. Any friend of Silas or those Jablonskis is a friend of mine."

We close the distance to the cabin and he ushers us inside.

"Sorry, I ain't got any sap on the boil, but I'm cooking down a bit of syrup to make some maple hard candies."

Taking a step forward, I mean to start my interrogation, but Erick grips my arm and offers a nearly imperceptible headshake.

I'm not pleased, but I comply.

"So, how'd the sap run for you last year?"

Ezekiel looks directly at Erick and tilts the large pot of syrup to check something—I have no idea what. "The first run was a mite disappointing. But I know what I am, you know. I'm not here to compete with the big boys north of the border. I got a nice little business here, and I got no problem with keeping it local, eh?"

Erick rubs a thumb along his jaw and nods as though he's been in the maple syrup business all his life. "Sounds about right. You ever run into Carol Olsen?"

Ezekiel narrows his gaze and strokes his thick salt-and-pepper beard. "You accusing me of something, Sheriff?"

"Absolutely not, Mr. Elhard. As I said, this is not an official visit. I'm sure you heard about the discovery Sunday morning. Miss Moon was the one who found the body."

Once again, I watch the man's expression soften like melting ice. "Well, I sure am sorry to hear that, Miss. Although, I can't say as Carol didn't get what was coming to her."

Erick nods. "What makes you say that?"

"Well, this is the time o' year all the barrel rollers set up their contracts with sugar makers. Now, I don't get involved, mind you, 'cuz I run my own operation. Less hands in the pot, less hands in the till."

The sheriff smiles and nods exuberantly. "Ain't that the truth."

This *hick-afied,* man-of-the-people Erick is really tickling my funny bone.

"That there Carol Olsen didn't see things that way. She was always clawing her way up the tree, you know? She thought she could get some contracts up Québec way, but the big boys didn't like her tapping into their sugar bush. If you know what I mean?"

Erick nods as though he knows exactly what Ezekiel means, while I've only managed to puzzle together bits and pieces.

The key point seems to be that Carol was sticking her nose where it didn't belong, and some powerful maple syrup titans took her out.

Sheriff Harper glances toward the pot. "Looks like you hit the sweet spot."

Ezekiel strokes his beard and glances into the pot. "Good eye, Sheriff. If that lawman thing doesn't work out for ya, there's always a place for you in my sugar shack."

Erick thumps him hard on the back and smiles. "Sure do appreciate that. Let me know if you think of anything else."

"You betcha."

We turn to head out of the shack, and Ezekiel calls after us. "Hold on. It's not gonna be as good as a real sugar off, but you may as well get yourself a little taste while you're here, Miss Moon."

He takes the large stainless steel pot off the fire and scoops a ladle in, then squeezes past Erick and me to pour an arc of hot, thick syrup in the snow. Returning to the hut, he hands us each a tongue-depressor-size craft stick. "Dig in."

Erick shows me the simple technique of rolling the cooling maple syrup mixture onto a stick. He pops it in his mouth and smiles like a child at a carnival. "Wow, Ezekiel. There's no question in my mind why Odell won't serve anything but Sweet Harbor Maple at the diner."

The flavor is rich, caramelly, mapley, brown sugary, and maybe even a little vanilla-y. It's beyond delicious. "Thank you. It's really a treat."

He smiles and nods his thanks. As we head back toward the stand of maple, he calls out, "Keep an eye out for that bear on your way back. She tends to come runnin' when she smells the maple."

I stop with my stick of maple sugar goodness in my mouth and stare at Erick in terror.

He shakes his head. "Ignore him. He's just messing with you. Bears hibernate in the winter, Mitzy. We're safe."

Of course. I know bears hibernate in the winter. Even an Arizona girl like me knows that. There's no time to feel like an idiot though, because I'm too busy lapping every last drop of deliciousness off my little wooden stick.

CHAPTER 9

ON THE WAY back to the station, Erick places a call to dispatch. "Yeah, see if you can get Clermont on the phone and send Johnson to pick up Wayne Olsen for questioning. 10-4."

"Who's Clermont?"

He grins as he taps end on his cell. "Would you believe he's a Canadian Mountie?"

I offer a slow clap as my response.

He glances at the road ahead, turns and offers me a quizzical stare. "Why am I getting the slow clap?"

"Because, in all the time I've known you, I've secretly imagined you as *Dudley Do-Right*. It makes perfect sense that you would have connections with the Canadian Mounties." Tapping my thumb on the steering wheel, I click my tongue. "It's kismet."

He rolls his shoulders back and sighs. "Look, I don't have Canadian Mountie friends. I have a single friend, who I've known since I was a teenager, who happens to be a Mountie. Him and his dad used to go hunting with me and Odell. When you're hunting moose through dense forest, sometimes you lose track of borders. It was always nice to have a tag that was valid in the US and one that was valid in Canada."

"True confessions of a juvenile delinquent." My heart warms with imagined memories of Erick and Odell's adventures. "You were lucky to have Odell in your life. Do you think it was his influence that pushed you toward joining the Army?"

Erick's gaze flows toward the horizon, and his mouth opens twice before words come out. "I don't think so. I was proud to serve my country— But who's to say? He was probably the strongest male role model in my life. He made sure my mom got an occasional break, and he definitely taught me the value of a hard day's work."

"Did you ever work at the diner?" I can't explain what popped into my head and shot that question out of my mouth, but the expression on Erick's face practically screams—

"Uncanny, Moon. I suppose that was one of your random hunches." He shakes his head and mumbles another "uncanny" under his breath.

"So, that's a yes?"

Erick nods. "Yeah, I was no good at waiting tables, but I was a rock star in the pot shack." His laughter is easy and soft.

"Um, what's a pot shack?"

"Sorry, Army jargon. It's where the dishes get scrubbed."

"Copy that."

At the intersection, he points toward the station. "You want to drop me at the station, or are you coming in?"

Smiling broadly, I tilt my head and nod. "You know, Sheriff, you're really starting to get the hang of this partnership. When you muscled your way into my sugar shack shenanigans, I thought I'd lost control of this investigation. It's nice to see that I'm still at the helm."

"I'm not inviting you to run the investigation, Moon. I'm inviting you into the station, to sit in my office while I place a phone call. If history has taught me anything, when I step into the interrogation room to talk to Wayne Olsen, I don't have a lot of control over who comes and goes from the observation room."

"You're not wrong." I park on the street and enter the station behind him. He heads off to change back into his uniform, while I take a moment to greet the deputy at the front desk, whom

I've nicknamed "Furious Monkeys" due to her obsession with said app on her phone.

True to form, she is lost in coconut combat.

"Hey, Baird. How's that game treating you?"

"The new levels are definitely getting harder. They've added blue bananas, which may or may not explode, depending on how you pick them up."

I'm not going to touch that information with a ten-foot pole. "Copy that. What level are you?"

"306. First one in my region to get there. Treehopper17 is hot on my tail, though. I'll probably lose the number-one rank by tonight."

I have no idea how to respond to that tidbit of information, so I smile and sashay through the crooked wooden gate. As it swings closed behind me, the lone deputy in the bullpen looks up.

Shoot. I was sincerely hoping to avoid a confrontation with schoolyard bully, Deputy Paulsen.

She pushes back from her dented metal desk and gets to her feet. The position doesn't increase her height a great deal, since she's a short, squat individual. Her right hand is poised on her gun handle, as per usual. "Ran across another body, eh, Moon?"

The woman gets under my skin. I just can't help it. "Looks like it. Someone's got to do your job."

Before she can access a snappy response, I hustle into Erick's office.

He's behind the desk, exchanging pleasantries with his childhood hunting buddy, Clermont.

"Hey CC, I want to put you on speakerphone. She just walked in." Erick gestures to one of the uncomfortable wooden guest chairs. "Mitzy Moon, I'd like you to meet Charles Clermont, CC for short."

"Bonjour, mademoiselle."

My heart unexpectedly skips a beat. "Hi. I thought Erick said you were Canadian? Are you from France?"

His lyrical French accent sings from the cracked plastic speaker on Erick's desk phone. "No, mademoiselle. I am French Canadian, from Québec. I understand you are dipping your fingers in our syrup. Pray they do not get bitten off by these maple badgers."

I want to respond, but the hum of his beautiful accent has completely thrown me off my game.

Erick leans back and his fingers tap rhythmically on his wooden desk. "Looks like she's having a little trouble with the accent, CC. Dial 'er back a notch, eh?"

"No problem, Harper. What do you need?" The Mountie's thick French accent is reduced by easily fifty percent.

The sheriff looks at me and nods with satisfaction. His momentary flash of jealousy evaporates. "Clermont neglected to mention that he's married to a very nice American woman. They lived in the states for five years and he was with me on one of my tours in Afghanistan. When he returned, they settled in Canada and he joined the Mounted Police."

"Thank you for your service, Mr. Clermont."

He chuckles warmly. "Call me CC."

"Copy that, CC."

Erick fills him in on the recent homicide and the victim's suspected involvement in less-than-legal maple syrup trade. "So, we were wondering if you could look into Carol Olsen's passport history and give us a timeline for the last couple of weeks. If you have any CCTV information or other leads that might explain her whereabouts prior to the murder, I'd sincerely appreciate it."

Clermont chuckles. "Would you consider it a personal favor, Harper?"

Erick points to the phone and shakes his head. "Listen, CC, I saved your bacon more than once over in the wasteland. Don't make me remind you about the details."

"Yes sir, Harper, sir."

"Knock it off. How soon can you get the info?"

"End of day, latest."

There's a brief pause and I give Erick a lame thumbs-up. Not sure why.

"You and your—"

"Girlfriend, CC. She's my girlfriend."

"Excellent. You should come up to Québec for a weekend getaway."

I lock eyes with Erick, and, sadly, we both laugh out loud. I field the question. "Yeah, we've tried the getaway thing, but Harper thinks I'm a corpse magnet. You probably don't want that kind of trouble in your country."

CC chuckles. "This isn't your first—what do you Americans say?—rodeo?"

"It is not. If I were to use maple syrup terms, I'd say you could label me Grade A sleuth material."

He laughs warmly. "I do look forward to meeting you one day, mademoiselle." The accent kicks into overdrive on that last word.

Erick rolls his eyes and picks up the receiver. "That's enough flirting with my gal for today, Clermont. Update me as soon as you can."

The call ends and he drops the receiver into the cradle.

"He seems nice."

Sheriff Harper stands and scoffs. "You'd be surprised how many ladies have uttered that phrase in my presence. CC is a hopeless flirt, but he's one hundred percent faithful to his wife."

The comment seems to impugn my honor, so I jump to my feet. "What exactly is that supposed to mean?"

"Nothing. Trust me, I wasn't saying anything about you. I've never been suave, or whatever. I suppose I was always a little jealous of his 'game.'"

Placing my hands on my hips, I offer a hula-girl swirl and then gesture from my head to my toes. "Well, I don't care how much 'game' he has. He didn't land all this, did he?"

Erick laughs and tenderly scoops me into his arms. Before he can plant a kiss on my ready lips—

Loud exhale. "Johnson put Wayne in room two, Sheriff." Paulsen groans as she waddles back to the pen.

"I feel like I have to say, 'wait here, please.' I'll see you after I finish this interview." Erick stands in the door and smiles down at me. His big blue eyes are full of affection, with a hint of exasperation.

"And, I feel like I have to say, 'copy that.'"

He steps across the hall and the door to Interrogation Room Two clicks open and softly closes.

Creeping toward the doorway, I check that the coast is clear.

All clear.

I slip across the hall, step into the observation room, and click the silver toggle on the speaker.

Erick sits calmly across from Wayne Olsen. If the setting were anything other than an interrogation room at a police station, you'd think the two friends were enjoying a beer and discussing sports. Unfortunately, this is a murder investigation and Erick has to ask his old friend some tough questions.

"Wayne, we've known each other a long time and you are more familiar than most with police procedure. I've got to ask these questions, and I need you to answer to the best of your ability."

"I understand, Harper. No hard feelings."

"Where were you Saturday evening between 8:00 p.m. and midnight?"

"I was at Twiggy's for supper and a nightcap."

"Did you leave the house at any point before morning?"

Wayne shakes his head. "It's impolite to kiss and tell, but I left shortly after breakfast. Probably around 8:15. Maybe a little later."

"Were you aware that Carol Olsen was in the area this weekend?"

Wayne leans back and his hands grip the edge of the table. He swallows hard and takes a deep breath. "I know how this next part is going to sound, Harper, but you asked me to answer honestly, and that's what I intend to do."

"Much appreciated, Wayne. Continue."

"As you know, I've made more than one attempt to divorce cagey Carol. She's contested at every turn, and dragged things out for years. Saturday, she showed up at my place suddenly willing to sign papers."

For a moment Erick forgets he's the sheriff conducting an investigation and reacts like a good friend. "That's great news. I know you've been trying to move that forward for over five years."

Wayne nods and presses his lips together with regret. "I wish it were that simple. She had conditions."

Erick's spine straightens. "Go on."

"Not sure if you keep up to date with my old man, but his health has been failing rapidly. My mother finally convinced him to take early retirement, and they made the big announcement Friday at a small gathering out at their place. Everyone was relieved, and even my father looked the picture of health as the burden was lifted."

The sheriff nods encouragingly.

"The problem is, that burden goes straight from his shoulders to mine. I wasn't exactly eager to take over. I never wanted the crown, and I've been telling him as much for years. He tried to sell the business a few times, but never got an offer for what he thought it was worth. The current medical situation kinda forced my hand."

"Well, I'm sorry to hear that. Are you going to try to run it?"

Wayne shakes his head and shrugs simultaneously. "I can't even wrap my head around that right now, Harper. This whole thing with Carol has really knocked me off balance."

Erick steers the interrogation back on track. "You mentioned conditions. So Carol showed up, willing to move forward with the divorce, but she had conditions. Can you elaborate?"

"Absolutely. She told me that this is what she'd been waiting for. Now that I had officially inherited the business, she'd happily grant me a divorce for half."

The sheriff leans forward, and I can easily imagine the shock on his face, even though he's seated with his back to me. "Half? She wanted half of a business she had nothing to do with?"

Wayne's shoulders sag. "That was just her opening move. What she really wanted was for me to buy her half out. For some reason, she thought my father was loaded. She assumed I'd inherited the business and a mountain of cash. Carol always was a misinformed dreamer. Dangerous combination."

Erick leans away from the table and exhales. "You're right. This does look bad. Your ex-wife shows up, attempts to extort a sizeable chunk of cash from you, and winds up dead within twenty-four hours. I really hope your alibi holds up under scrutiny."

Wayne's jaw drops and his kind eyes widen. "What are you saying, Harper? It's the truth. I was with Twiggy. I know it may not make me sound less guilty to admit I technically spent the night with my mistress while my wife was being murdered, but you know the situation with Carol."

Erick nods and pushes his chair back. "Thanks for coming in today, Wayne. We'll follow up on the details of your story, and I'll be in touch." He steps out of the room, and Wayne's head drops into his hands.

From where I'm sitting, every bit of his story rang true. He and his wife had been separated for years, and if he'd actually had anything to do with her death, it's unlikely he would've shared the details of a private conversation. No one knew about Carol's attempt to extort money from Wayne, except him and the deceased. The fact that he shared that detail with Erick goes a long way toward supporting my belief that he's innocent.

Back in the sheriff's office, I can tell this case

isn't sitting well with my boyfriend. "You don't think Wayne's guilty, do you?"

He tips back in his dilapidated office chair and laces his fingers together behind his head.

Old habits die hard, and my gaze darts toward his abdomen, in the hopes that his shirt may come untucked and I'll get a peek at those washboard abs.

My compulsion offers a little comic relief, and he winks at me lovingly. "Thanks for being here. It's tough to separate my friendship with Wayne from my duty, but I have to. If it were anyone else, that story would absolutely make him look more guilty. But his alibi seems to line up with Twiggy's, and he had no reason to tell me that story about Carol trying to get money. I don't think a guilty man would give me that kind of ammunition."

Leaning forward, I put my elbows on the desk and nod in agreement. "That's exactly what I was thinking. Him and Carol were the only ones who knew about the conversation. If he was guilty, it would be foolish to share that detail."

Erick leans in, reaches across the desk, and grips my hand. "Thanks. Something just doesn't sit right, though. I can't quite put my finger on it."

"Go on now, Sheriff. Don't be trying to steal my *hunch* thunder."

He laughs and rubs his thumb along the back of my hand as he quietly ponders the case.

True to form, a thought pops into my head, and I blurt it out. "Wayne mentioned his dad retiring and not wanting to take over the business. What kind of business is it?"

"The Olsens are the founders of Crimson Crest."

I scrunch my shoulders up and tilt my head. "And?"

"Oh right, some 'locals only' knowledge. Crimson Crest Cranberry Farms is a locally owned grower and processing operation. Folks say they have the best bogs in the north."

As soon as he utters the word cranberry, I lean back in my chair and try to ignore the circle of heat emanating from the mood ring on my left hand. I don't have to look at it to know that it's going to show me an image of the garland tacked to my murder board.

"I know that look, Moon. Spill."

"I thought it was nothing. Pyewacket stole a strand of homemade garland from Isadora's tree. He chewed up all the popcorn pieces and only left the cranberries. Then he brought it to me and attacked me when I tried to throw it in the trash."

Erick crosses his arms, momentarily distracting me. "That cat is as uncanny as you. What do you think it means?"

"Well, we know Carol wasn't killed by cranberries. But maybe we're looking at this from the wrong angle. Maybe it wasn't a maple syrup connection."

His jaw muscles flex as he grinds his teeth. "I'm afraid that only makes things worse for Wayne."

"Accurate."

CHAPTER 10

WHEN I RETURN to the bookshop, Stellen is waiting outside the front entrance, carefully examining the intricate carvings on the antique wooden door. The look on his face is all too familiar. "What do you think? Is it Pyewacket?"

He glances up from where his fingers are tracing the outline of a fiendish feline and grins. He walks me through the details of the ornate vignettes. "This one is Chiron and Hippodamia. This is Pegasus with a nod to Selene, and here is Pan and the gift of Aphrodite." When his hand reaches the carving of the wildcat, he crouches and leans his face close to the timber. "This looks like a caracal. It actually looks a lot like Pyewacket. Seems like there are even scratches over the left eye. Do you think it could've been added later?"

"By whom? Supposedly Silas found this door in San Miguel de Allende, Mexico, and had it shipped to Isadora as a grand opening gift. Maybe he bribed the carver to make changes or additions?"

Stellen chews the inside of his cheek and shakes his head. "Everything displays the same degree of weathering. There's honestly nothing that shows any of the carving was done at a different time. Puzzling."

Nodding my head, I slip the hefty, one-of-a-kind brass key out from under my shirt and tug the chain over my head. Inserting the triangular barrel into the cleverly concealed plug, I spin the key three times and feel the lovely sensation of, not just the lock, but also the entire store opening to my touch.

"Speaking of puzzles, come on up to the apartment. This case is turning into a real doozy, and I could use your genius brainpower to my advantage."

"The Carol Olsen murder?" He frowns.

"The very one." I hope working on the case won't stir up unpleasant memories for him.

Stellen holds the door for me. His mother, who died too young of an aggressive cancer, raised him right.

Grams joins us in the apartment, and I serve as afterlife interpreter, while she writes up additional cards for me, and fires off questions about Stellen's freshman year at college.

When all is said and done, the addition of the cranberry inheritance has tied way too many green strands of yarn between Wayne and Carol.

"Far be it from me to question the great and powerful Robin Pyewacket Goodfellow, but I'm having a problem understanding how a woman who's trading in possible black-market maple syrup is murdered by something to do with cranberries?"

Grams hovers above the stack of index cards and nods in agreement. Stellen lies stretched out on his stomach on the floor, scratching rhythmically between Pyewacket's tufted ears. "Did you mess up this time, buddy? Is a cranberry just a cranberry?"

"Ree-ow." Soft but condescending.

Stellen looks at me and shakes his head. "You know him better than I do, Mitzy. Sounds like he's doubling down on his cranberry clue."

The alliteration makes me giggle. Ghost-ma and Stellen stare at me in confusion.

"Cranberry clue? You guys didn't find that funny? Maybe it's just me and my desperate need to deflect with humor."

Stellen tilts his head to the side and scrunches up his face. "Doesn't really seem that hilarious to me, but maybe you have to be older."

I squeeze my eyes to slits and stare daggers at

the little smart aleck. "Are you calling me old? I'm maybe five years older than you, if that. Be careful who you're calling old, punk."

He rolls over on his back, and Pyewacket immediately takes the opportunity to lie across his chest and pin him playfully to the ground.

"Traitor." I scoff and shake my finger at the spoiled cat.

Grams floats toward the murder wall and examines each name and tidbit of evidence carefully. "I'm sure Wayne didn't do it, dear. Although, I have to admit the evidence is piling up against him."

Striding toward the board, I pluck one of the strands of green yarn like the string on a cello. "That's exactly how I know he didn't do it."

Stellen lifts his head and stares at me over the tan lump of his master. "Can you break it down for me, sis? That doesn't make sense."

"No problem. As an expert in film and television, I've watched far more footage than anyone has a right to. The first thing you learn about mysteries of any kind is that the suspect who looks the most guilty by the second act is never—I should say extremely rarely—the guilty party. So, I know things are piling up against Wayne, but I'm not going to fall for it. I know that the update from Erick's Canadian Mountie contact is going to shed new light on this."

No one chimes in to praise my clever sleuthing.

"And I'll apologize in advance to Pyewacket, but I just don't think it has anything to do with the cranberry connection."

Stellen laughs so hard it disturbs his royal furriness, and Pyewacket is forced to seek solace within the thick down comforter on my antique four-poster bed.

"Now what's so funny?"

"Cranberry connection! I get it. I hear it now. It is funny."

Rolling my eyes, I flop onto the settee and stare at my phone. Willing it to ring.

When the phone actually rings, all three of us, including the ghost, jump with fright.

"It worked! I made the phone ring."

Stellen stares at me and swirls his hand in a "get on with it" motion. "Good for you. Now answer it."

"Right." It's Erick, and he has an update from CC. "Great. I'm going to put you on speakerphone so Grams and Stellen can hear the news. We're all in my apartment working on the murder wall." I tap the speakerphone icon and Erick's voice fills the room.

"Of course you are. Why would I believe for even a split second that this investigation was solely in the hands of the Pin Cherry Harbor Sheriff's Department?"

"It's so cute when you think you're in charge. Now, dish."

Grams floats toward the phone and Stellen sits up straight.

"CC checked with the Border Services' records and noted seven crossings for Carol Olsen in the last two weeks."

"So she was definitely doing something in Canada. Was he able to get any leads on who she was meeting or why?"

"He was. There was some CCTV footage of her meeting with a man known as Antoine Berg-eron, a notorious barrel roller who is way up the food chain. CC said the footage didn't have any au-dio, but it looked like a heated argument. Maybe she was working for Bergeron, or maybe she was poaching in his territory."

Grams glows expectantly. "That sounds good, sweetie. Is it?"

Nodding, I continue. "Grams thinks that's promising. What about this Antoine guy? Was there any evidence that he came into the United States?"

Erick clicks his tongue and sighs. "Unfortu-nately, a man like Bergeron doesn't do his own dirty work. If he sent someone to take out Carol, we'd have to comb through two weeks of Border Ser-vices' records to find the lead, and that's assuming the assassin bothered to enter by legal means. You know what that border is like. He or she could've snuck across anywhere."

"I suppose. Do you have a picture of this Bergeron guy?"

There's a pause on the other end of the line. The tapping of fingers on a keyboard is the only sound. "I took a screenshot of the CCTV footage. It'll be a little blurry, but that's all we have."

"All right. We'll keep looking at our end. I know Wayne's innocent. There's got to be something we're missing. Stellen and I are going to head over to the diner to fuel up for an all-nighter. Can you meet us?"

I gesture to Stellen, and he jumps up, confirming my suspicion that teenage boys are always hungry.

"I can't get away right now, Moon. Say hi to Odell for me and let me know if either of you get any *hunches*."

Ending the call to the sound of Erick's laughter, Stellen and I head for the diner.

CHAPTER 11

ONCE INSIDE MY home away from home, we grab
the booth in the corner, and Tally hops over with
her standard-issue grin in place. "What can I
getcha?"

"I'd like a mug of hot chocolate and . . . a cinnamon sticky bun."

Her eyes widen. "No fries?"

I tilt my head and ponder the question. "No.
No fries."

Glancing back at the kitchen, I take note of
Odell's smug grin and the lack of bubbling oil in the
fryer. He knew! How does he always know?

Stellen orders hot chocolate and a slice of pin
cherry pie à la mode.

As Tally gets our order together, Odell saunters
out. "How's the case going?"

"Not great. The more we dig, the more evidence we find that makes Wayne look guilty. I wish we could find one thing that would put him in the clear."

Odell tilts his head. "Did his alibi check out?"

"Hard to say. Twiggy is his alibi. As much as I hate to say it, she could be covering for him. I know I'd cover for someone I cared about."

He turns without a response, retrieves the *Pin Cherry Harbor Post* from the counter, and slaps it on our table. "This may not put Twiggy in the best light, but it oughta clear Wayne." Pointing to the large photo above the fold, he taps in the center.

There, in the middle of the Northern Lights Yuletide Extravaganza, which took place Saturday night, is Wayne Olsen lighting the tree in the central square.

"What time is the tree lighting?"

"It's usually at nine o'clock every year."

"Well, if he was in the town square, lighting the town Christmas tree at 9:00 p.m., he certainly wasn't having dinner at Twiggy's place."

Stellen stares at the picture and shakes his head. "You're right, Odell, this might clear Wayne, but now Twiggy doesn't have an alibi."

Odell shakes his head and raps his knuckles on the Formica twice before returning to the kitchen.

We finish our sugar power-ups in silence and

head straight out of the diner, make a right-hand turn, and trudge into the sheriff's station.

No one is manning the front desk, so we help ourselves through the gate and head back to Erick's office.

He looks up and smiles. "Hey, guys. How's college treating you, Stellen?"

My stepbrother mumbles, "Not too bad."

Erick gets to his feet and comes around to meet us. "You two look pretty forlorn. Is this a hunch, or worse?"

"Worse." I shove the Sunday paper into his hands and point at the photo. "Correct me if I'm wrong, but that looks a lot like Wayne Olsen, lighting the tree at 9:00 p.m. sharp on Saturday night."

The sheriff looks at the photo, tilts the paper back and forth in the light, and chews his bottom lip. "It does look like Wayne. It's not a clear picture of him, though. The tree seems to be the thing in focus."

Nodding, I cross my arms and step back. "That's the artistic eye of Quince Knudsen for you. I know for a fact he takes multiple exposures of every shot. Maybe he changed the focus on some, too. Stellen and I will head over to the newspaper office and see if he has any other shots."

Erick nods. "You know how bad this makes Twiggy look, right?"

"Yeah. We thought of that. I mean, all kinds of folks at the Extravaganza will be able to vouch for Wayne." Attempting to employ my feminine wiles, I step closer to Erick and place my hand on his arm. "Don't do anything until we talk to Quince, all right?"

My clairsentience instantly informs me of his increase in heart rate. Looks like I've still got it.

The sheriff nods. "You have one hour."

"That's fair."

Stellen and I beat a hasty retreat before I can say anything to ruin our brief reprieve.

On the way to the newspaper office, I have to call Twiggy. She may be rough around the edges, but she's the only employee I have, and she knows a hundred times more about running that bookshop than I ever will. "Hey, I'm sure you're busy, but I thought I owed you a warning."

She makes one of her usual wisecracks, which I ignore in favor of giving her a heads-up about the alibi avalanche headed her way. "So, now that the picture of Wayne has surfaced, the sheriff is going to be calling your alibi into question, and that puts you back on the suspect list. Not to mention poten-tial charges for impeding an investigation."

I'll spare you the details of her swearing a blue

streak. The true meat of her argument is that she didn't lie. Wayne was at her house for dinner and did spend the night.

"All right. Fine. I wanted you to know what was going on. We're headed over to the newspaper office now to see if I can get a better picture for Sheriff Harper. I want to help you out, Twiggy. Are you telling me I should lose the negatives?"

When I mention losing the negatives, Stellen twitches in his seat. Sure, I've pulled some questionable moves in his presence in the past, but I did promise Silas to keep it on the up and up around my little brother. I'm supposed to be setting a good example, not teaching him how to be a better delinquent. Apparently, I had a temporary backslide. Not to worry. Twiggy immediately refuses my offer and tells me to do whatever I think I need to do. She's got nothing to hide.

Ending the call, I glance at Stellen. "She's so exasperating! I wasn't actually going to destroy evidence, though. You know that, right?"

He nods, but his face says he seriously doubts my backpedaling.

The great lake that dominates our region commands its own intricate weather system. When we step out of the Jeep and head across the street to the home office of the *Pin Cherry Harbor Post*, an icy wind whips through town and sends the tempera-

ture plunging an easy twenty degrees in the negative. The moisture in my eyes creates tiny icicles on
my eyelashes in the space of seconds.

Lucky for us, the front doors are open. Stellen
and I burst inside, desperate for shelter.

Despite the progress that visits the rest of the
world, nothing has changed in this town that tech
forgot. The birch-clad reception counter still displays an antique silver bell and a sign instructing
visitors to ring for service.

However, this isn't my first visit to Pin Cherry's
fourth estate. I slip behind the counter and walk
through the doorway into the office area. Stellen
follows silently.

Photojournalist, and possibly friend, Quince
Knudsen, isn't at the desk. He must be in the
darkroom.

Like a lot of things in this town, he's clinging to
the past with his 35mm film, photo enlargement
apparatus, and tried-and-true developing methods.
The proof is in the pudding, though. The national
wire services have picked up his amazing images a
multitude of times, and his impressive portfolio certainly helped him get accepted into Columbia Uni-
versity.

Stepping into the black metal cylinder, I motion
for Stellen to wait as I disappear inside the magical
tube and rotate the door around me. A sliver of red

light expands to fill the barrel as the powerful odor of acids and ammonia hits me. "Quince, you in here?"

"Yah."

I'm not sure what he's learned at the impressive college, but it certainly wasn't conversational skills. Quince has a talent for monosyllabic responses, and it appears today won't be anything out of the ordinary. "I need to buy some prints off you."

"Cool."

He's the best. Easily motivated by financial incentive, Quince has helped me out more than once. When I figured out that his currency was literally currency, it was easy to make arrangements that served both of us nicely.

"Yeah, cool. I need to know if you have other angles from the Christmas tree lighting Saturday night. I'm willing to look through some contact sheets if you have them."

He makes some adjustments on the enlarger he's working with, sets the timer, hits a button, and steps back as light passes through the negative and exposes a piece of photographic paper beneath. "Nope."

"Nope, as in you don't have a contact sheet? Or nope, as in you don't have any other angles? Or nope, as in—"

"Dude. Nope, as in no photos."

I almost consider this pile of words a soliloquy, but I still find the message confusing. "Look, Quince, I'm not here to cause trouble. If you're trying to protect Wayne, Erick will have to get a warrant and press charges for impeding an investigation. I know you have photos. I saw one above the fold in Sunday's edition."

Taking the photo paper from the enlarger, he slides it into the first chemical bath of the three trays set up in his stainless steel developing run. He taps the timer on his phone and turns toward me with an unreadable gaze. "I didn't take pictures."

"Oh, all right. Does your dad take digital photos or does he use a film camera like you?"

Quince's phone beeps, and he turns back toward the developing process. Grabbing a pair of rubber-tipped tongs, he pulls the sheet of paper out of the first solution and slips it into the second, tapping another timer on his phone.

"Neither."

"Quince, I know this song and dance is part of our thing, but I really need a better picture of Wayne Olsen lighting the Extravaganza Christmas tree. Can you help me or not?"

He crosses his arms and flicks his long sandy-brown bangs backward with a jerk of his head. "There was a snowstorm in Chicago. My flight was delayed. Dad was putting the edition together and counted on me to get the pictures."

I hesitate to interrupt his abnormal flow of words, but curiosity gets the better of me. "You said you didn't take photos."

"Right. We had to run last year's picture. You know how everything stays the same around here. Same people, same clothes, same everything. No one noticed. Until now."

Stellen grips my arm and I nearly jump out of my skin. I was so absorbed in extracting information from Quince that I didn't realize my stepbrother had followed me into the darkroom. "Yeesh! You're too quiet for your own good."

For some reason, that makes Quince chuckle, which makes Stellen chuckle, because Quince was always one of the cool kids at school and Stellen certainly wasn't.

Stellen's extra brainpower and early graduation were a blessing in disguise. He's definitely hitting his stride at college, and he's going to make an amazing veterinarian. "You two know each other, right?"

Quince bobs his chin. "Hey."

Young Stellen tries to play it cool. "Hey."

I roll my eyes in the semi-darkness. "Anyway, what's on your mind?"

He smiles, and his teeth look pinkish-red in the

light. "That means Twiggy was telling the truth. And so was Wayne. The photo was from last year, so their alibis still hold up."

I throw my arms around him and squeeze his scrawny shoulders. "And that's one more for the genius! Those of you keeping score at home, be sure to mark that down."

Stellen looks at the ground, shrugs, and heads back to the cylindrical door.

I turn to follow.

A hesitant voice calls out. "Hey, you need those prints then?"

Classic Quince. I'm getting hustled, and this kid is as good as Emma Stone in *Easy A*. Reaching into my pocket, I grab a couple of twenties and lay them on the counter next to the enlarger. "Thanks for your time, *dude*."

He walks toward the crumpled bills, and when I step into the cylinder to spin my way out, I hear him utter, "Sweet," as he pockets the cash.

CHAPTER 12

BEFORE RETURNING to the station to share my update with the sheriff, I drop Stellen at the bookshop. "Update Grams, and, if it's not too much trouble, you can apologize to Twiggy for me."

Stellen shakes his head and steps back to close the passenger door.

Ducking so he can see my face through the closed window, I press my palms together and plead.

He shakes his head again, this time with more conviction, and dusts his hands to show he's taking no part in my possible feud with Twiggy.

Oh well. It was worth a try. I'll take my lumps when I get back.

Activity has picked up inside the station, and Paulsen is barking orders like she runs the place. To be clear, she has run for sheriff in Birch County twice, but my handsome, over-qualified boyfriend defeated her soundly both times.

My suspicion that the team is pulling together in hopes of finding a break in the case is confirmed when I see Furious Monkeys fielding phone calls and taking copious notes. If Paulsen found a way to get Deputy Baird to put down her cell, things must be serious.

Taking advantage of the portly Paulsen's preoccupation . . . I won't even try to say that five times fast. I slip into Erick's office and grin mischievously.

He looks up from the report on his desk and frowns. "I don't like that look. You're up to something. Do I want to know what?"

"I have some good news. Not that it helps our case, but it helps our friends."

He crosses his arms over his powerful chest and takes a deep breath. "Oh, it's *our* case now, is it? You must need a favor."

"Rude." Scoffing, I wave away his insult with a flick of my wrist. "I thought you would appreciate the fact that I was making an effort to work together. But if you want me to keep my intel to myself, I'm happy to do so, Sheriff."

"We've come too far, Moon. You're in the inner circle now. Whether you were invited or not is a topic we can debate at a later time."

I roll my eyes and plunk onto the open chair. "You may be interested to know that Quince Knudsen did not take pictures Saturday night."

Erick runs a hand along his jaw and furrows his brow. "Please tell me there's more to the story."

"Oh, there is. No one took pictures Saturday night. The elder Knudsen was at the newspaper office putting the edition together, and Quince's flight was delayed. They had to run a shot from last year. Last year! So, Wayne wasn't at the extravaganza this year, he was at Twiggy's, like they both said."

Erick smiles briefly and smacks an open hand down on his desk. "I knew it. I knew Wayne would never lie to me. Thanks, Moon."

"No problem. I'm as relieved as you are. I was making all kinds of justifications for Twiggy's dishonesty, but, the truth is, it didn't sit well."

He nods, picks up a pen, and taps the end rhythmically on his desk. "I'm gonna call CC and find out if he's had any luck locating Antoine Bergeron."

"Yeah, I don't like the look of that wily-eyed Bergeron rascal. He has one of those creepy grins that shows too many teeth and pushes his cheeks up like two baked potatoes. I'm sure he has something to do with this."

"What is it with you and potatoes?" Erick picks

up his phone and dials the Canadian Mounted Patrol. "Sit tight."

I wait calmly in the uncomfortable chair, but under no circumstances am I sitting tight. I don't even know how to sit tight. What a foolish expression.

"Hey, CC. It's Harper. Is it okay if I put you on speakerphone again?"

The Mountie must've consented, because Erick taps the button and the sultry voice of the French-Canadian spills from the speaker. "Bonjour, mademoiselle."

Without meaning to, I immediately take on a terrible French accent and respond. "Bonjour, monsieur."

CC laughs louder than I feel is necessary. "Not bad, Mademoiselle Moon. But you really must come to Québec and put in the proper amount of practice if you want to improve that accent."

Erick offers me a stern look, and I sit back in my chair like a chastised child.

"We're running out of suspects down here, CC. As we go down the list and confirm alibis, it's looking more like this may have been the work of an assassin hired by somebody on your side of the border."

"If Madame Olsen fell afoul of maple syrup law, then you could be right. However, I have tapped my contacts to the limit, and I can find no concrete evidence that she made any inroads. I have confirmed meetings, I have confirmed arguments, and I have images of her at various sugar makers. What I do not have is a shred of evidence that any of those sugar makers signed a contract with Madame Olsen. Perhaps she was, how do you say, shaking the trees? But I fear nothing fell from those bare branches."

The mood ring on my left hand turns to ice, and I glance down in time to see a hand twisting a silencer onto a gun barrel. "Um, CC, do you know if Antoine Bergeron owns a gun with a silencer?"

He ignores my question and immediately addresses Erick. "Harper, have you recovered the murder weapon?"

Erick raises one brow and eyes me suspiciously. "We have not. However, I've learned to give Miss Moon's hunches fair credence. Do any of the images you have of this Antoine character show him with firearms?"

CC makes a sound that is a cross between blowing a raspberry and outright spitting. "The man is no amateur. He would never brandish a firearm. And, as I mentioned, it is quite likely he would hire someone to do his dirty deeds. He hasn't worked his way to the top of this food chain to take unnecessary risks."

"10-4. Thanks for the interdepartmental cooperation, buddy."

"Not a problem, Harper. I think it's my turn to take the moose, no?"

Erick laughs and leans toward the phone. "The rules haven't changed, CC. I can't help it if I'm a better marksman than you." Erick ends the call, leans back, and continues to tap his pen in frustration.

"You said the shot was too precise to be an amateur or an accident. What if you're wrong? What if Carol and someone were out in the woods to find a Christmas tree, just like us? Maybe the person with her brought a gun for protection, from wolves or whatever, and maybe it went off by accident."

He drops his pen, pushes his chair back, and gets to his feet. "That's as good as any other theory we have right now. I'll get the deputies to round up any of her acquaintances or people she might've had dealings with in the last couple of weeks." He takes a step toward the door.

My blurt button trips and I ask, "Did Wayne say what his father was suffering from?"

Erick's eyes dart back and forth as he scans through his memory of the interview. "No. He just mentioned a progressive medical condition, and his father's need to retire. I don't remember any details about the diagnosis."

Slowly getting to my feet, I tap a finger on my lips as I toy with my next move. "Maybe we should talk to his father. I know it's not really anything to go on, but it's all I can think of right now."

Sheriff Harper nods. "I think Johnson's on that side of town. I'll ask dispatch to pass along the request."

By the time Deputy Johnson returns to the station, I've talked myself out of Wayne, or his family, having any connection to Carol's murder. However, I'll be keeping my doubts to myself. Erick stuck his neck out by bringing a man in for questioning based on a feeling I had when I couldn't think of anything else. The last thing I'm going to do is leave him holding an empty bag.

I'm posted up in the observation room with an ice-cold can of caffeinated pop and a bag of tortilla chips. Nothing would complete this snack better than some freshly made salsa, but what passes for Mexican food at this northern latitude hardly fits the bill.

Erick opens the door for Mr. Olsen, and an elderly man with thick white hair hobbles in, supporting most of his weight with a four-pronged cane. He eases himself into the chair facing the observation room, and Erick takes a seat with his back to me.

"Mr. Olsen, I appreciate you cooperating with our investigation."

"Nonsense. Anything to help our local law enforcement. And call me Niklas."

"Of course. I'm sure you've heard about the passing of your daughter-in-law, Carol. I hope you understand, we're speaking to everyone who knew the victim, just to rule them out. You're not a suspect. I hope you will be forthcoming with your responses."

Niklas Olsen considers the speech carefully and nods. One hand rests in his lap, the other still grips the knob atop his sturdy cane. "She was my daughter-in-law by technicality only. You know how many times Wayne tried to untie that knot. I'm sorry she met with a violent end, but I'm not sorry she's gone."

Setting down my bag of chips, I lean forward and take several deep breaths. There was something in that phrase, something that triggered a spark in my extrasensory perceptions. It's time for me to stop snacking and pay attention.

"I appreciate your honesty, Niklas. Were you aware that Carol had entered the country from Canada several times in the last two weeks?"

He looks directly at Erick as he answers. "I was not."

Erick makes a note on his pad and continues. "When did you decide to retire?"

"I made the announcement Friday night, out at the old compound, as Norma calls it."

"Yes, sir. I understand you had a family gathering Friday evening. What I'm asking is when did you make the decision to retire? A man in your position can't have taken a move like that lightly. I know how hard you worked to expand your business and remain independent from the big conglomerates. Transitioning things to a new company president would take time to organize. What I'm asking you is how long has Wayne known about your plans to retire?"

Niklas grips the top of his cane and adjusts his position in his chair. His gaze narrows. "My boy had nothing to do with this, Sheriff. If you brought me in here in some sort of underhanded attempt to get me to incriminate my son, you've made a grave mistake."

Erick places his notepad and pen on the table and glances across at the elder Olsen. "Niklas, you know I think the world of Wayne. I don't think he had anything to do with this, but if the information has been public knowledge for several months, other people may have found out about your plans.

Someone could've been blackmailing Carol, knowing she'd have access to the Crimson Cranberry coffers."

To his credit, Niklas Olsen doesn't laugh. I can't say the same. Alliteration amuses. I've giggled at accidental alliteration since I was a kid.

Niklas lifts his hand from his lap and places it on the table. I note a slight tremor.

"Sheriff, the decision was more sudden than I care to admit."

I sense Erick's desire to make a note in his notepad, but he admirably resists. "May I ask about your diagnosis?"

"Why not? Everyone will know soon enough. I have Lou Gehrig's disease. I'm on a whole slew of medications, and I'm working with a physical therapist to preserve my diminishing muscle strength for as long as I can. But for all their degrees and certificates, the doctors can't tell me anything definite. There's not much peace of mind in being told you're suffering from a progressive disease with a time horizon that could span anywhere from a couple of months to five or ten years."

Erick leans back and exhales. "I'm so sorry. I had no idea. Is that why Norma pushed for your retirement? For your health?"

The energy in the room shifts, and an odd spark of light twinkles in the old man's eye. "Boy, I've read the stories in the papers about some of the cases you solve. But sitting right here, across from you, and watching that fine mind of yours at work— Well, it's a real treat, Sheriff."

From my vantage point in the observation room, I'd say that was a movie-trope-classic deflection.

Luckily, Erick is easily as smart as he looks. "I appreciate the compliment, Niklas. But I need you to answer the question."

The elderly gentleman chuckles and nods in defeat. "Norma did insist on the retirement, but the medical issues were only half the reason." He lifts his proud chin, stares Erick in the face, and refuses to break eye contact.

I have the advantage of my psychic senses to pluck the word *affair* out of the ethers, but I have no explanation for Erick's genius.

"I know the business was doing well financially, and that only leaves me with one solid option. Were you involved with someone at work?"

Niklas Olsen's jaw drops and, despite his condition, his hand claps loudly on the tabletop. "Well, I'll be—"

"Was Wayne aware of this . . . indiscretion?"

The light in Mr. Olsen's eyes fades and his shoulders droop. "He was not. And out of respect for my family, I'd appreciate that it stays that way, Sheriff."

Erick nods once. "If it's not pertinent to the investigation, Niklas, I see no reason to make it public. Can you tell me the woman's name?"

Niklas Olsen eases his chair back, re-grips his cane, and struggles to his feet. "I cannot. My apologies, Sheriff. Some things just need to stay between a man and his wife."

As Niklas reaches for the door handle, Erick tries for one more piece of information. "How long, Mr. Olsen?"

The defeated man turns. "What are we talking about? The affair or the retirement?"

Erick slowly gets to his feet. "I'd like to know both."

"The affair has been going on, in one form or another, for almost ten years. The retirement was planned hastily, about two weeks ago at the most. Wayne only found out Friday night."

Mr. Olsen turns the handle and opens the door. As he shuffles out, Erick thanks him for his time.

My head is buzzing with questions.

Erick taps on the one-way glass and points toward his office.

CHAPTER 13

AFTER I NOD MY HEAD, it occurs to me he can't actually see me, so I scoot across the hall and take my seat in one of the visitor's chairs.

"Any hunches, Moon?"

The question catches me off guard. "Hunches? What are you talking about? There's no way that old guy hiked into the woods, in knee-deep snow, and shot someone."

He brushes away my distracted thinking. "No, of course not. I was referring to the woman he was having an affair with."

"Oh, that." I rub my hands on the thighs of my skinny jeans, close my eyes, and take a deep breath.

Erick attempts to slip quietly into his ancient office chair, but it squeaks mercilessly under his weight.

Focus. Focus. Focus. I coach myself into a state of semi-calm and a name pops into my head. I angrily dismiss it and try again.

Same name.

Throwing my hands up in exasperation, I blow a raspberry and lean against the chair. "It's no use. I just keep getting the name Carol. And unless there's something really strange going on in that family, I don't think there's any way Niklas Olsen was having an affair with his daughter-in-law."

Sheriff Harper grabs a pen and doodles on the back of a piece of paper. His wheels are turning, my wheels are turning, but we seem to be stuck in the Bog of Eternal Stench. Nothing like a good *Labyrinth* reference to lift my spirits. "I have an idea."

Erick's pen stops before he lifts his gaze, but, when our eyes meet, I can already see his objection. "I'm pretty sure I'm not gonna like this, but I'm also rather familiar with my inability to stop you, Moon. Might as well tell me. Forewarned is forearmed."

"I'm working off the theory that there's no better way to catch up on company gossip than working at said company. So, I'm gonna run home and slip into one of my business suits, snatch a pseudonym from thin air, and apply for a job at Crimson Crest Cranberry Farms. Whaddya think?"

"I don't know what to think. Sounds like a bad idea, but I've seen you get out of stickier situations."

"Great." I slap my knee enthusiastically. "So, we're all in agreement. I'll check in tonight at dinner. My place or yours?"

He launches to his feet and closes the distance between us. Strong arms circle around my back and pull me close.

My tummy tumbles all over itself.

"May as well take advantage of my mom being in Florida. Why don't you head over to my house tonight and let me cook you dinner?"

"Clearly, you know the way to my heart, Sheriff."

He bends down so that his lips are brushing against mine as he whispers, "I'm hoping to find my way somewhere else."

And I'm dead.

Thankfully, his strong arms keep me from collapsing as my knees turn to jellyfish beneath me. I offer him a quick peck on the cheek and race out the door before he can observe the crimson cranberry red of my cheeks!

The door of the bookshop closes behind me with a hollow echo.

"Grams? Grams, where are you?"

Twiggy stomps out of the back room and holds her hands up in a frozen "shrug emoji" pose. "Are you seriously yelling to the ghost of your dead grandmother? What if there were customers?"

I take a hesitant glance between the stacks. "Are there?"

"No, I'm just sayin'."

"Point taken. Also, you're one hundred percent off the suspect list. In case you're wondering."

Twiggy crosses her arms and shakes her grey pixie cut. "No. I wasn't wondering at all."

"Fair enough. I'm headed out to apply for a job at Crimson Crest Cranberry Farms, so if you've got any tips on how to pick up gossip . . . You didn't hear it from me, but apparently Wayne's old man has been having an affair for about a decade. He wouldn't name the woman, and—"

Twiggy turns to tromp her biker boots out of sight, but calls over her shoulder, "And you couldn't resist an opportunity to snoop. You're not gonna find anything out there. But, a word of warning, stay out of the sights of Miss Tremblay. She may only hold the title of executive secretary, but she acts like she runs the darn place."

"Thanks for the tip." I lift my leg to climb over the chain at the bottom of the spiral staircase as Grams rockets through the wall from the printing museum in a delayed response to my summons. Her sudden appearance throws me off balance, and

I tumble from my precarious perch onto my ample backside. "Perfect timing, Grams."

Twiggy's cackle echoes from the back room. Apparently she's seen me fall handle over spout enough times that just the sound of impact is enough to tickle her fancy.

"What's so urgent, sweetie?"

"I'm going undercover." I offer her a pair of finger guns and she rolls her translucent eyes.

"Is it dangerous?"

Easing myself over the chain, I fill her in as I climb the treads and saunter across the Rare Books Loft.

"I'm not surprised to hear about the father's affair. The son, Wayne, is a doll, but have you met his mother?"

"No. I only learned her name today. Do you and Norma have a history?" I chuckle mischievously, because I honestly can't think of anyone in town that doesn't have a history with one of the many incarnations of my busybody grandmother.

"I'm not a busybody, Mizithra. I have good ideas and the courage to share them."

"And the audacity to never stop eavesdropping. Get out of my head, woman!"

We proceed directly into the massive closet, and Grams grabs the tried-and-true standard. Charcoal-grey Donna Karan pantsuit, but this time she pairs it with a cranberry-red silk blouse.

I gesture to the outfit. "I see what you did there. Nice touch. Is that some kind of subtle, subconscious color manipulation?"

She spins away from the shoe rack and gazes at the outfit in confusion. "What?"

"The cranberry-red silk blouse. Is that some kind of subconscious visual manipulation? Like, I'm wearing the color of their company, so I seem like a good hire?"

She scoffs. "I hadn't drawn the connection. Apparently I'm getting so good at this stylist career, I'm unconsciously competent."

"Oh brother." Donning the interview pantsuit, I head toward the exit.

"Do you have your secret identity?"

"For the record, it's a cover story, not a secret identity. I'm a snoop, not a superhero. And yes, Darcy Bergeron."

"I'd say you're beating a dead horse re-using that 'Darcy' moniker again, but I suppose the two names work nicely together. Do you have your resume?"

"My resume? The one that would simply have a list of coffee shops I worked at, and was fired from?"

"You're going for a job interview, Mitzy. Most people would take a resume."

"Well, I'm not most people, and I don't actually want a job. I'll make up some story about how I, Darcy Bergeron, just moved to the area, and haven't had time to get my printer set up." I flourish my fingers and take a shallow bow.

Grams claps her hands together gleefully. "You really are good on your feet, dear. Such an admirable trait."

I walk toward the intercom and press the plaster ivy medallion that opens my secret bookcase door from inside the apartment, chuckling as I leave. I think my grandmother just complimented me for being a good liar.

Crimson Crest Cranberry Farms is a much larger operation than their quaint, hand-painted wooden sign would imply.

The main office building is a sprawling ranch-style, which calls up images of the 1960s. Between the parking lot and the building stands a ten-foot-high decorative latticed-brick wall. They framed the windows with plain aluminum frames, and the only difference between this building and some vintage architecture in the Southwest is the peaked roof. I've learned a great deal about the weight of snow since I arrived in almost-Canada, and improperly reinforced flat roofs can be a real disaster under two or six feet of snow.

The sidewalk leading up to the main entrance has been shoveled and salted. Lucky for me! I may only be wearing a two-inch heel, but my severe lack of coordination wouldn't survive an icy patch, even in tennis shoes. The double doors are painted red, and the left one seems to be secured.

Taking a deep breath, I grab the handle of the right-hand door and review my backstory.

Darcy Bergeron. Just arrived in town from—Québec! Thunderbolt and lightning. I love it. I'll be a French-Canadian. I'm fairly confident I can mimic CC's accent well enough to make it through a fake job interview.

Confidently opening the door, I walk toward the reception area on my right.

No modern birch and steel here. There's a large glass window with a small hole for conversation, and a scooped cutout at the base where she slides the clipboard through. "Please sign in here, and indicate who you're here to see."

The receptionist has a youthful face, with wide-set eyes. Unfortunately, her overly back-combed hairdo ages her prematurely.

French accent engaged. "But of course. I am

here to complete the job application. This would be human resources?"

She's not impressed with my French flair. "Do you have an appointment?"

"Sadly, no. This was not possible. I must get a new chip for the local phone service."

She exhales and lifts the receiver of her large tan desk phone. "Have a seat. I'll see if Edith can squeeze you in."

Dropping into one of the faded blue vinyl chairs, I kick myself mentally for choosing a French backstory as I grab a magazine to distract myself.

The privacy glass may prevent someone who's hard of hearing from picking up on the patronizing tone in the receptionist's voice, but me and my extra senses can hear it clear as day.

The woman is not a fan of people who don't follow the rules. However, based on the hint of disappointment as she ends the call, I'd say that Edith has found a way to shoehorn me into her schedule.

The thick wooden door leading from the lobby into the bowels of the establishment opens with a loud click. A wisp of a woman with a jet-black bob and cat-eye glasses on a chain peers into the waiting area. "Ms. Bergeron?"

Swallowing my snarky instinct to point at myself in shock and look to the empty chairs on the left and right, I turn on the accent and reply. "Yes. Thank you so much for agreeing to see me."

She presses her frail body against the door, and, for a moment, I worry she may lose the battle and be knocked off her feet. "Right this way."

I walk past her and pause on the threadbare blue carpet in the hallway.

Edith closes the door and heads left down the hall. Just before she's about to pass through a doorway that T's into another hall, she makes a sudden left and steps up into the human resources office.

I follow her and she gestures to a chair much like those in the lobby, but less faded.

She takes a seat in her brand-new ergonomic office chair, and for a moment I can't get over how out of place it seems in the historic setting.

"Ms. Bergeron?"

Whoops. I've heard that tone before. I must've zoned out and missed her first, or possibly even her second, query.

What's the French word for sorry? "Pardon."

"I was saying we'll conduct the interview first, and then if I think you might be a good fit, you can fill out the paperwork. That'll save both of us some time. What do you say?"

"Oui, this is wonderful."

"So, did you move here from France?"

"No, no, Québec."

The look on Edith's face shocks me. I'm certain Québec is an interesting town, but I seriously doubt it's worth the shock and awe I'm currently witnessing.

"You're French-Canadian?"

I nod and smile, just like my mama taught me. "Oui."

"Oh, gosh. I know this is unorthodox, but you just have to meet someone. Follow me. It will only take a minute."

Who am I to argue with a woman who may offer me a job at this fine establishment?

We retrace our steps under the harsh fluorescent lighting, and the worn carpet seems to begrudge the visit. As she passes the door to the lobby, I glance into an office on our left and stifle a gasp when a massive painting of a creepy, possessed boy in a sailor suit looms into view. Finally, she makes a left-hand turn down a wide carpeted hallway. The quality of the floor covering here is an obvious step up from the main walkway.

We pass two setups, each with a secretary's desk on the left and a large office on the right. We've clearly entered the executive area of the Crimson Cranberry.

As we reach the end of the spacious hall, an attractive blonde in her mid to late forties walks out of the large office and pinches her lips together with irritation.

Edith appears suddenly flustered. "Oh, Miss Tremblay, I'm so sorry to bother you. Darcy is French-Canadian! Just like you. I thought you'd like to meet."

Miss Tremblay crosses her arms and strums perfectly manicured fingernails on her right bicep. "We don't all know each other, Edith. Is this woman selling something?"

Before Edith can answer, Miss Tremblay pushes her way past us and takes a seat at her desk.

The mumbled response from Edith as she struggles to cool Miss Tremblay's wrath fades away as though I've suddenly slipped below the surface of a bath. All sound is muffled when my eyes lock onto the golden nameplate on the executive secretary's desk.

Carol Tremblay. Carol! That's the name that kept popping into my head in Erick's office, and now I know precisely why.

There's no more decisive exit than intestinal disorder. I grab my stomach with both hands, lurch forward, and cry out, "Sacré bleu!"

Beating a hasty retreat, I grab the handle on the large door leading to the lobby and run out through the exit before the cranky receptionist has time to formulate a question.

CHAPTER 14

TEARING out of the Crimson Crest parking lot, my Jeep fishtails and I struggle to employ the counter steering method my dad taught me. I finally get the vehicle under control, but barely.

I'm so excited about my discovery! I'll never make it back to town with my secret intact. Pulling to the side of the road, I nudge into the six-foot drift left by the snowplow and text Erick the news. "I know the woman's name."

The electric thrill of uncovering the critical clue tingles through my veins as I wait for my phone to ping with a response.

Instead, I'm gifted with an actual phone call.

I put the call on speaker and look over my shoulder to pull back onto the rural highway. "Hey, are you as excited as I am?"

My lead foot is the wrong method for moving oneself out of a snowbank, and my tire spins.

"Um, do you have any tips for getting out of the ditch?"

Erick chuckles. "You need to ease off the gas pedal. Work your tires back and forth in a zigzag, and once you get a little traction give it some gas."

I follow his instructions and, just as my tire grips the road, a white Land Rover rips past me at a totally unsafe speed. "Holy *Fast and Furious*, Batman!"

Erick's voice instantly fills with concern. "What happened? Are you all right?"

"Yeah, luckily I didn't lurch too far into the roadway. Some insane person just blasted past me at about a hundred miles an hour."

His breathing is uneven. "Are you sure you don't want me to send a tow truck?"

The tires finally grip the salted roadway like they mean it, and the Jeep swings back onto the plowed road. "I got it. It's all good. Sorry for the unnecessary segue. Are you ready to hear my news?"

He laughs. "Yeah, I've been ready. Some say, I was born ready."

"Well, that's debatable. Here are the highlights." I bring him up to speed on the undercover operation and the sudden need to be French, and he scoffs unnecessarily. "What? I can do a passable

French accent." In case he doesn't believe me, I treat him to a sampling. "Bonjour, monsieur."

"Get to the point, Moon."

"Right. It's a good thing I decided to be French, because as soon as the human resources lady heard my accent and discovered I was French-Canadian, she had to introduce me to someone. That someone turned out to be Niklas Olsen's executive secretary."

"And . . ."

"And, besides the fact that she's a real 'B,' would you like to guess her name?"

He pushes a loud breath through his teeth, and I can tell he's nearing the end of his patience. Time to put a bow on this story.

"Her name is Miss Tremblay, also French-Canadian. And her first name is—wait for it —Carol!"

The shouts of praise and the standing ovation I expect do not follow.

"Did you hear me? Her name is Carol."

"I'm not following."

"Yeesh! Remember in your office, when I was trying to see if I had any hunches about the woman Niklas was having an affair with?"

"Oh, right. Looks like your hunch was spot on, Moon."

"This is what I'm saying. She seems super

sketchy. I think you should bring her in for questioning."

"On what grounds?"

"I don't know. I'm not trying to tell you how to do your job."

This comment brings gut-busting laugh-out-loud hilarity from the normally sedate sheriff. "Oh, is that right? What exactly are you telling me to do?"

"Well, if I was the sheriff, and this was my investigation, I guess I'd bring in Miss Tremblay to see if she had any additional information about—"

"Mmhmm. I'm waiting, Moon."

At last, the bolt of psychic inspiration hits. "About his retirement! He claims he only decided to retire in the last two weeks. If that's true, his executive secretary would absolutely be able to confirm, or deny."

"Excellent work. I'll send Paulsen out to pick her up."

"Paulsen? Why would you pick her?"

I can hear the smile in his voice. "Well, you said this Carol Tremblay is a real 'B.' So, I figure we fight fire with fire."

I have to cover my mouth to keep the laughter from bursting his eardrums. "Erick! I don't think you're supposed to talk about your employees that way!"

"Easy, Moon. I only said it to get a rise out of you. Paulsen may be a handful, but she is one of the most effective deputies on my force. I'll take high-spirited over unmotivated any day."

I sense his comment refers to present company, not just his star deputy. "I'll take that as a compliment."

"Are you coming into the station, or headed back to the bookshop?"

"Back to the bookshop to get changed. Plus, I have to update Grams and the murder board. When you get Carol in the interrogation room, fire off a text."

"10-4."

Back at the bookshop, Grams is thrilled to hear the not very lurid details of Niklas Olsen's affair. She eagerly fills out a 3 x 5 card for Carol Tremblay and I tack her on the board, completing the update by running the yarn from Wayne to Niklas to Carol Tremblay. I have no way of knowing if Carol Tremblay was acquainted with Carol Olsen, so we leave that link off the board for now.

But Grams makes a question mark card that I tack between the two Carols.

Glancing at my phone, I make a rough calculation for how long it would take Deputy Paulsen to drive out to the cranberry farm and back. "They should have her by now. I don't understand why Erick hasn't texted."

"You're a modern woman, dear. You can always text him."

"How avant-garde."

We both giggle, and I type up a simple text requesting an update.

For the second time today, my text results in a phone call. I'm not thrilled with this repeat break in protocol, but I do love the sound of his voice. "Hey, Erick. You're on speakerphone with me and Grams. What's up?"

"That vehicle that sped past you . . . Is there any chance it was a white Land Rover?"

I look at Grams and send her a quick telepathic message. *Do you think he's psychic?*

Grams giggles and rolls her eyes.

"It was. How would you know that?"

"Because, when Paulsen got to the farm, Carol Tremblay was nowhere to be found. We ran her name through the motor vehicle database to uncover the make and model of her vehicle. The receptionist said that Carol left suddenly with no explanation. I just put two and two together. Trouble is, we have no idea where she is now."

"You've checked her house or apartment?"

"Moon, not my first day on the job."

"Sorry, of course you did. How can I help?"

There's a pause and click in the background that may be a door closing. He lowers his voice and whispers into the phone, "Can you do your pendulum thing?"

"Oh, sure." I look at Grams and shrug while she grins maniacally and claps her hands. "Give me a few minutes to get set up, and I'll call you back when I have a location."

"Thanks. And this is just between us, right?"

"Who am I gonna tell?"

He chuckles and ends our call.

"Battle stations, Grams."

I push the secret panel beneath one section of the built-in wall of bookcases in my apartment, and a large drawer pops open. As I'm digging around to find the pendulum, the corner of a manila file folder catches my attention and brings a surge of guilt. It happens that I permanently borrowed Isadora's medical file from the records room at the local hospital one time when I worked undercover. My fingers curve around the pendulum and interrupt my remorse.

"Grams, I know I apologized once, but I'm sure it doesn't hurt to offer another one. I'm not exactly sorry I stole the records, but I am sorry I looked at them without your permission."

Her disinterest seems an act. "It's fine, dear."

She generally doesn't use such a short, clipped

tone with me. "Grams, I'm so sorry you and Odell lost your baby. It must've been a lot to deal with in such a new marriage."

She busies herself, straightening her strands of pearls and adjusting the many rings on her fingers. "Yes, it was difficult when we lost that one."

"What did you say? What do you mean, 'that one'?"

She zooms toward me, grabs the Birch County map from the drawer, and whizzes toward the coffee table. "The deadline, young lady. There'll be time to discuss family matters later."

When she mentions *Family Matters*, all my psychic abilities fly out the window as I put on my best Urkel impression. "Did I do that?"

Her laughter is halfhearted. She doesn't even look at me. All her attention is focused on smoothing the map out as perfectly as possible on the coffee table.

Seems like this is one of those times when it's best to let sleeping dogs lie. I shake the pendulum, letting it twist back and forth and sort itself out as I approach the map. "Do you think there's anything special I need to ask, or just where is Carol Tremblay?"

Grams taps one of her ring-ensconced fingers on her coral lip. "I think you're going to have to be more specific. You know how Silas gets."

"Boy, do I!"

As Grams and I huddle over the map, Pyewacket becomes spellbound by our actions.

He approaches the map, reaches a needle-clad paw toward the edge, and attempts to yank it onto the floor.

"Pye! This isn't a game. I'm trying to find someone."

He makes another, more determined attempt, and to my surprise Grams swirls toward him with uncharacteristic ire. "Robin Pyewacket Goodfellow! You stop it this instant. You are spoiled absolutely rotten!"

Wow. I've never seen her talk to the cat that way. "All right. Everyone calm down. I need to focus to make this work."

Pyewacket sulks into the closet, and Grams hovers opposite me.

Inhaling deeply, I attempt to clear my head. I extend my arm over the map and let the chain settle. Once the room is quiet, and everything inside my head is still, I focus my energy and ask my question. "Show me the current location of Carol Tremblay and/or the woman who drove past me in the white Land Rover this morning."

This version of the question seems to please the powers that be. The pendulum starts slowly, but quickly spins in larger circles, like the chair-swing ride at a carnival.

On previous occasions, when I watched Silas, the pendulum made two or three arcs and then pulled toward a specific location on the map. This time, the arcs seem to get wider and wider. It's almost as though the pendulum is reaching—

Grams speaks my thoughts out loud before I have a chance to formulate them. "I think you need to move it closer to the edge of the map, Mitzy. It seems to be trying to reach farther than the current radius."

I move my hand slowly in the direction that feels right, but the pendulum continues to circle wider, stretching farther.

I move my hand a little more.

Still pulling.

I move my hand a little farther.

The tip of the conical stone jerks toward the far edge of the map. As it hits the paper, it pulls even farther. Staring at the compass symbol, I'm mesmerized by the letter "N."

Grams and I lock eyes and shout in unison, "She's headed for Canada!"

Grabbing my phone, I call Erick and give him an update.

The news invigorates his investigation. "Thanks. Gotta go. Gotta call CC."

I collapse against the thickly padded back of the settee and exhale. "That was crazy. I've never felt the thing pull like that. There's so much to learn about my powers, and alchemy, and the energies in the universe . . ."

Grams floats toward the map like a feather on a gentle breeze. Her ethereal arm stretches out and one shimmering finger points to the edge of the map where the pendulum hit and dragged.

I lean forward and both of us giggle at the same moment. There, right on the northern border between Birch County and Canada, is a hole and a tear. The kind of hole made rather recently by a caracal's claw.

"Come out, come out, wherever you are, Pye. You're a genius. I'm a stupid human. All hail Pyewacket the wise."

And, as if on cue, he struts out of the closet with his tufted ears held high. He glances at the ghost of Grams, which we've both decided he can see, and then his gaze settles on me. To say that it's the smug look of an overlord gazing upon his subjects would be frighteningly accurate.

I raise both my hands in the air and mockingly bow down to the amazing Pyewacket. After three or four bows, he seems to accept my apology.

"Re-ow." Thank you.

Now that our urgent business has been handled, my grandmother's earlier comment has to be addressed. "Grams, I know you really don't want to talk about it, but I think you should. What did you mean by 'that one,' when we were talking about the child you miscarried?"

She freeze-frames and flickers like the tracking lines on an old paused videotape.

"Grams?"

A moment later, she pops out of the visual spectrum.

"Oh no you don't! You don't get to avoid this conversation, Isadora."

Having learned her weak spots in the past, I head into the closet to threaten her precious couture.

Inside the hallowed walls, I make my threat. "Myrtle Isadora Johnson Linder Duncan Willamet Rogers, you're acting like a human child. If you don't pop into this room immediately, I'm going to start a small designer label bonfire."

She rockets into the room with such force, I fall backward onto the padded mahogany bench. "Yikes! Take it easy."

Ghost-ma swirls toward me, filled with compassion. "Are you okay? I'm so sorry, dear. I know the clothes aren't important. In my heart, I know relationships are more valuable than fashion, but there's still a tiny part of me that can't let go of the glamor of haute couture."

"I'm fine, Grams. As you know, we Duncan women are well padded."

We share a chuckle, but the bright glow of love emanating from her fades as sadness shrouds her energy.

"You can tell me anything, Isadora. I know we tease each other, but I would never judge you. I've done plenty of things I'm not proud of in my short lifetime. Please, trust me with the truth."

She slowly circles the large closet, running her ghostly fingers along the lush array of fabrics. "Odell was my first true love. I had plenty of crushes before him, and there was an undeniable attraction to Cal, but I believe Cal was far more sure about the future of our relationship than I was. Before I could make a decision, they both enlisted in the Army, and Odell came back first."

"Are you saying it was more convenient?"

She hesitates and touches a simple gold band on her left ring finger. "I'm saying it was fate. Fate sent Odell to me, and we were blissfully happy. When Cal came back, things just turned so awful, so fast. He and Odell were fighting, and I mean fisticuffs, not just words. I tried to escape it all in a haze of whatever bottle was in the cupboard."

"So you divorced Odell and left the country?"

"Not exactly. I just left the country. Odell filed for divorce a few months later."

"Oh. And when did you meet Max?"

"I met Max the moment my plane landed in Paris. He was waiting for someone in the terminal, and either they didn't show up or maybe their flight was delayed. I took one look at him, dressed to the nines, European good looks, and an aura that screamed money—"

"Geez. That's a heckuva change from down-to-earth, small-town Odell."

She sighs. "I tend toward the dramatic, dear. I thought I could erase him through grand gestures and over-the-top behavior. Max was the perfect fit. We jet-setted all over Europe, married a month later, and drank our way from Latvia to the Greek Isles. It wasn't until that fateful car crash that either of us ever took our foot off the gas."

Emotions are swirling, and my inappropriate humor takes over. "No pun intended, I'm sure."

She looks away from the Oscar de la Renta, tilts her head, and offers a wan smile. "Oh, I didn't realize what I said."

"Sorry, Grams. You know how I get. Continue."

Her head droops. "Well, you know most of the rest of the story. Once I sobered up, I came back to Pin Cherry Harbor. I was determined to set things right with Odell and send Cal packing.

But I came back to a completely different situation."

Her story draws me in, and I lean toward her.

"Odell had pushed the divorce through in my absence and wouldn't speak to me. Cal was eager to pick up where we had left off before his stint in the Army. Mostly, I was lonely and confused."

"So you married Cal and started a family. Why do I get the feeling there's a huge piece of the story I'm missing?"

"Because there is." Her shimmering ghostly eyes seem to look through a portal into the past. Designer-clad shoulders sag, and ghost tears spring to the corners of her eyes. "I couldn't let go of Odell. I had to make one enormous last attempt."

The hairs on the back of my neck are tingling, and an icy chill from my mood ring tempts me. I'm not going to dive into my psychic powers to uncover her secret. It's important that she tells me herself. "It's all right, Grams. You can tell me."

She drifts toward the padded bench and the hum of her energy brushes my skin. "I got pretty drunk. I made sure Odell did as well."

Uh oh. I've heard one too many stories that started like this. In fact, I've had a starring role in a few.

"We spent the night together, and, in the morning, I thought it would be easy to convince him to give me another chance."

"Why wouldn't he? It's obvious how much he loves you. He never remarried."

"He blamed himself for my relapse. Odell said we just weren't meant to be, and he never forgave himself for betraying his best friend. He and Cal had been best friends, before and during their days in the Army. Of course, all that changed after."

"So things didn't work out with Odell, and you ended up marrying Cal. It wasn't terrible, was it? You said your days with Cal and Jacob were some of the happiest of your life. Wasn't that true?"

"It was true, mostly. I made the best of a tricky situation. I maintained my sobriety, by living a lie."

The hairs on the back of my neck are stiffly on end, and my mood ring screams to be acknowledged. Taking a deep breath, I hold her gaze. "What was the lie?"

"Cal wasn't Jacob's father."

The room seems to be shrinking. I feel dizzy and I can't swallow.

She wraps her ghostly arm around my shoulders and tries to shake me. The connection with the intense emotion of the situation robs her of the ability to take corporeal form. "Mitzy? Mitzy, are you okay?"

"Are you saying what I think you're saying?"

"Probably. What do you think I'm saying?" Her luminous eyes look toward the plush carpet and tears spill over her cheeks.

"Odell is Jacob's father? Odell isn't my surrogate grandfather. He's my actual grandfather?"

The weight of what she's telling me is almost too much. I curve toward Ghost-ma, and reach out to comfort her, but she vanishes from the visual spectrum.

Sliding down to the floor like maple syrup pouring over the edge of a table, I lie against the soft carpet and stare up at the cedar-lined ceiling.

Thoughts, images, and emotions race through my body. What should I do first? Should I go talk to Odell? Should I tell my dad that the man he grew up thinking was his father isn't? It's all too much.

I squeeze my eyes closed and dream of escape. Unfortunately, the ringing cell phone in my pocket has other plans.

CHAPTER 15

WHEN ERICK'S name pops up on the caller ID, for the first time I can remember, I don't want to answer.

In the end, my insane sleuthing gene takes over, and I answer the call on speakerphone. The mobile rests on my stomach, and my eyes gaze aimlessly at the ceiling as I mumble, "Hello."

"Mitzy, we got her. Are you in?"

"What? You got who?"

There's a pause, and Erick's voice softens. "Hey, are you okay? You sound weird, and you're also not telling me what to do. Should I call the paramedics?"

His gentle teasing reaches my wounded inner child, and I roll onto my side, sliding the phone closer to my face. "Um, I'm in a pretty weird place.

I can't really get into it. It's hella complicated! Maybe you should take this one without me."

The soft tone vanishes from my boyfriend's voice as he embodies the sheriff he truly is. "Listen up, Moon. I'll be there to pick you up in two minutes, and you are to accompany me to the border to recover the fugitive. Your tip led to this capture, and I refuse to let you miss out on your moment of victory because you're having a pity party. Suit up. I'm on my way."

He ends the call without giving me a chance to whine, complain, or cry.

Sitting up in confusion, I shove my feet into a pair of shearling-lined boots, grab a thick puffy jacket, and march downstairs, ready to give him a piece of my mind face-to-face.

The tires crunching over the icy snow in the alleyway alert me to his arrival, and I step outside. I'm working hard to shove my emotions down as I rest an impudent fist on my hip.

He steps out of the car, takes one look at me, and jogs toward me. A moment later, his muscular arms wrap around me like a snuggly blanket and he's kissing the top of my head. "I don't know what happened, but we've got a little drive ahead of us and I'm all ears."

Why did he have to be nice to me? That's the worst. Big salty tears plummet down my cheeks.

He kisses my lips and escorts me to the passenger side. Carefully placing me inside and securing my seatbelt, he hustles around to the driver's side and backs out of the alley.

As we drive past Pancake Rock, I get my silent tears under control. The gorgeous crests, curves, and caves in the ice floes on the shore of our great lake take my mind off my family drama for a moment.

"Hey, Mitzy, whatever happened, you can tell me."

His hand is on my knee and I reach out and grip his fingers as though they're a life raft on a raging ocean. "Erick, I don't want to tell you. I don't think I want to tell anyone."

His thumb caresses the side of my finger and his voice is tender. "You do. Trust me, Moon. Shoving it all down inside is the worst possible option. I tried that when I worked my way across the country, writing the names of fallen soldiers on the back of those green-and-white population signs at the edge of their hometowns. Sure, it kept me moving, and it kept the demons at bay, but it wasn't until I actually talked to someone about the pain I was going through that I found my way out. So, talk to me. It's what couples do."

He squeezes my knee as he utters that last phrase.

Deep down, I know he's being painfully honest. "All right, but I'm telling you this as my boyfriend. There's some stuff you might not approve of, and I don't want to get a lecture from Sheriff Harper in the middle of pouring out my heart. Deal?"

He nods. "Deal."

I race through the bit about me removing medical records from the hospital, and, to his credit, the only sign of disapproval is the flexing muscle of his clenched jaw. When I get up to today's conversation, a fresh sob temporarily interrupts my tale.

His large hand gently rubs my knee. "Go ahead. I'm listening. Finish your story."

Admitting Odell is likely my actual grandfather, and Jacob's biological father, is harder than I imagined. I get choked up a couple of times, and encouraging words and kind smiles from Erick are the only things that pull me through to the end of my story. "So, she just dropped that on me today, and vanished."

His bright-blue eyes fill with concern. "She crossed over? Permanently?"

I shake my head furiously at the thought. "No. I mean, I hope not. She just vanished out of the visible spectrum. Grams does that sometimes when she's mad, or, I suppose in this case, ashamed."

He puts both hands back on the steering wheel and gazes off toward the horizon point. "I never knew my biological dad. And me and my mother were okay with that. When you showed up in Pin Cherry, you met a father who you'd thought was dead. Look how things turned out for you and Jacob. I think it would be a mistake to keep this from him. Or Odell. But I'm no expert. Maybe you should talk to Silas."

"Yeah. Silas. That's a fantastic idea, Erick. Thanks for listening. Dagnabbit, my family is messed up."

He chuckles softly. "No more than anyone else's, Moon. You can only play the cards you're dealt. Talk to Silas. Then do whatever you think is best, and let's hope everyone can be an adult about this. Right?"

"Copy that."

I refuse to admit to Erick that his "talking about it" idea actually helped. But now that the emotional fallout has been sifted through, my snoopy nature is eager to hear more about Carol Tremblay's capture.

"So, did they stop her at the border?"

Erick smiles proudly. "I can't wait for you to meet CC. He pulled off a miracle today. There are a whole lot of people crossing the border during the holidays, and the Canadian government generally loosens restrictions, inspections, and stopping cars in general during these last two weeks of December. He had to move heaven and earth to reinstate the stop every vehicle policy. But it paid off! By the time he got down there with additional mounted patrols, the border services agents had detained three white Land Rovers, and secured Tremblay."

"Three! I had no idea that was such a popular car. And in white? What are the odds?"

He shrugs. "I guess the odds are about three in however many cars crossed the border today."

"Touché."

Erick reaches out his hand and I slip my fingers into his grasp. It's a strange sensation to be riding in a sheriff's vehicle, with a shotgun between us locked into the dashboard, and police chatter spilling over the radio, as we embrace this new level of bonding in our relationship.

Buildings, manned gates, and red and green lights loom into view.

"There's the border. We'll pull into this parking lot and let CC know we've arrived." Grabbing his phone, he calls the Canadian Mountie. "Hey, buddy. We're in the eastern lot, south of gate three." Erick listens intently. "10-4. We'll be right in."

He slides out of the cruiser, circles in front, and opens my door. "This isn't Pin Cherry, Moon. Please mind your manners, and act like you've been in the room before."

I take the offered assistance of his hand, step out of the vehicle, and toss my hair like every movie star removing a helmet in every movie you've ever seen. "So, no mention of breaking and entering, stealing evidence, and, I'm assuming, no accents?"

To his credit, he resists rolling his eyes. "Hang on to me. There's a solid layer of ice under this snow."

I'm not sure if his words are a generous offer to keep me from falling, or a thinly veiled threat. Maybe if I don't play nice, he'll let me fend for myself on the frozen tundra. I'm pretty sure I wouldn't last two minutes. Clutching his arm, I let a helpful mantra echo through my grey matter: Play nice. Play nice. Play nice.

The wind whips up and offers me a face full of chilly Canadian snow as we approach the office building.

Erick holds the door for me. Once inside, I stomp excess snow off my boots onto the industrial floor mat and swipe at my cheeks.

CC waves from a hallway and motions us through. "It's all right, officer, they're with me."

The woman, who looked as though she was about to mid-field tackle us, returns to her chair.

The tall, dark, and handsome man walks toward us. He's almost too good looking. In fact, he wouldn't look out of place on the cover of *Vogue*. His close-cropped dark hair and deep brown eyes complement his lithe form. Although, something about the way he carries himself indicates he can handle himself in a fight. Not because of brute strength, but lightning-fast reflexes.

CC nods to Erick and steps toe-to-toe with me. He grips my right hand, removes my mitten, and presses the back of my fingers to his perfectly curved lips.

Erick smacks him on the arm. "Simmer down, Clermont."

CC purposefully ignores his old friend, hands me my mitten, and slips my arm through the crook of his elbow as he escorts me down the hall. "Bonjour, mademoiselle."

I know I promised Erick, but there's something about accents—I can't control myself. "Bonjour, monsieur."

His playful eyes light up, and he nods his head in approval. The striking red jacket of the Mountie uniform is so much more impressive in person than it was in the old *Dudley Do-Right* cartoons. I'm honestly disappointed CC isn't wearing his Mountie hat. But, as I understand it, you don't wear those indoors.

He opens a door on the left-hand side of the hallway and leads Erick and me inside.

Erick glances around the small space. "Where's Tremblay?"

"Oh, she pulled the Canadian citizen card,

which dumped an extra ton of paperwork in our lap. Can I get you two some coffee while you wait?"

The mesmerizing lilt of CC's French-Canadian voice distracts me from his actual question.

Sheriff Harper pokes at me and shakes his head. "You in there, Moon? Don't be drawn in by his accent. He's married, and he's laying it on extra thick just to stick it to me."

Mentally smacking myself on the forehead, I attempt to follow orders. Right. Get it together, Moon. Sitting up straighter in my chair, I clear my throat. "I'd love some go-go juice, and a doughnut if you've got any floating around."

CC bows his head and steps out of the room.

Erick slides his arm around my shoulders, and I'm not entirely sure if it's for my comfort or to mark his territory. He tilts his head toward mine and whispers, "Do you want to step outside and call Silas?"

"Um, no."

He leans back as though I've offended him. "Sorry. I was trying to help."

"I didn't mean that as harshly as it sounded. It's a fine suggestion. But there's no way I'm stepping outside until it's time to run directly to the car. Which, if you love me as much as you say you do, you'll go out first and pre-warm."

He rolls his eyes dramatically and smirks. "Boy, talk about your Arizona desert princess!"

Crossing my arms, I turn away and pretend to be offended.

That's the exact moment CC chooses to return. "Oh, dear, this looks like a lover's quarrel."

Erick squeezes me a little tighter, and I snuggle into him for effect. The hum of his deep voice makes my skin tingle. "It's called a sense of humor, Clermont. Maybe you should get one."

CC and Erick share a chuckle, and I eagerly accept my black gold and a maple-glazed doughnut.

"I hope they made this glaze from real Canadian maple syrup. I'm told to accept no substitutes."

My quip catches CC off guard, and his comeback sticks in his throat.

My boyfriend smiles proudly. "Good one, Moon."

The Canadian Mountie recovers. "Let me check on the paperwork. We should have you squared away in five or ten minutes."

Erick and I enjoy our java and sugary treats in silence.

CC returns as I'm licking the sticky glaze off my fingers.

He smiles. "It is *that* good. And speaking of good, they're prepping her for transport now. I'll escort her to your cruiser, you'll sign the appropriate form, and the alleged murderer Carol Tremblay will be all yours."

Erick stands up as though CC has simply announced the time of day, but his phrasing catches my attention.

"Murderer? Did you find evidence she was responsible for Carol Olsen's murder?"

CC shrugs. "There was a weapon in her vehicle, which we bagged along with the other items, and you'll have to run ballistics, but she claims she's ready to confess it all. I hate to make your job too easy, Harper, but it looks like this killer is about to plead guilty."

Erick hands me his phone. "When we get her in the cruiser, I'll Mirandize her, and you hit record on the phone. If she's going to spill her guts on the ride home, I want a fully legal recording in our possession. We have no idea what her real involvement, or motivation, is. She may be cooperating in an attempt to stay in Canada. Once she's back in the good old US of A, she may change her story. Anyway, you've got my back, right, Moon?"

"Always and forever." The phrase leaps out of my mouth before I truly comprehend its meaning.

Both Erick and CC gaze at me with the same intensity.

The Canadian Mountie speaks first. "That sounds serious, my friend. I don't see a ring—"

I lift my left hand and display the antique mood ring bequeathed to me by my grandmother.

CC widens his eyes and stutters as he searches for an appropriate response. "That's, some— Well, it's— How . . . unusual."

A broad grin spreads across Sheriff Harper's face, and he offers me a sharp salute. "You are one in a million. Excellent work."

The Mountie gazes back and forth, and I put him out of his misery. "It was a gift from my grandmother. I wear it for the nostalgia. Although, I'm not exactly sure I'm willing to take it off, or replace it with something else. I've grown rather fond of it."

Now it's Erick's turn to look surprised, and CC's chance at a revenge chuckle.

"You two head to the cruiser. I'll bring Tremblay out in a flash."

Making our way through the swirling snow, I voice my concern. "What if she recognizes me from the fake interview?"

Erick pats my mittened hand as though he's comforting a child. "What if she doesn't? Why don't you let me handle things and focus on getting a clean recording of her confession? Sound good?"

It sounds ludicrous, but I keep that thought to myself. "Whatever you say, dear."

He groans and shakes his head.

Serves him right. You mess with the bull, you

get the horns. I mean, I'll try to behave, but my fourth foster dad always told me, "You play how you practice!" Of course, the joke was on him, because I always skipped basketball practice and I never played. Wait, maybe the joke's on me? Since it would appear I played exactly as I practiced—not at all.

CHAPTER 16

A GUST of wind pushes Carol Tremblay and a soupçon of snowflakes into the backseat. Erick and CC wrap up their business, shake hands, and give each other the infamous one-armed bro hug.

Carol sniffles and cries softly in the backseat. She hasn't noticed me yet, and for that I'm grateful.

Sheriff Harper hops into the driver's seat and signals me to start the recording on his phone.

He runs her through the standard Miranda warning, and I jockey the phone into position for the best sound capture. Flashes of the old days in film school, straining to hold a boom pole over my head as all feeling drained from my arms, bring a wistful grin to my face.

"Who is she?" Miss Tremblay leans forward

and, when she gets a better look at me, she gasps. "I saw you! You were at— Why—?"

My mouth opens, but the voice that fills the cabin of the police cruiser is Erick's. "Miss Tremblay, this is Mitzy Moon. She's a confidential informant for the Birch County Sheriff's Department."

My eyes widen, and I nod in appreciation. This Harper fellow is going places.

Carol presses against the backseat, but the panicked tone and rapid breathing continues. "But she's French-Canadian. What is a Canadian doing working for a United States sheriff's department?"

My lips can only stay locked for so long. It's blurting time, and I'm the one to do it. "My apologies for the subterfuge, Miss Tremblay. I'm not actually French-Canadian."

As the clipped words in my wholly American accent penetrate the grating between the front seat and the rear, Carol's weeping increases in intensity.

Glancing at Erick, I shrug. If anything, I would've thought my admission would have consoled her.

Erick ignores her tears and launches into questioning. "Miss Tremblay, is it true that you were having an affair with Niklas Olsen?"

Her tears stop abruptly and she gasps. "Yes, I guess, but how could you possibly know that?"

"I'm not at liberty to reveal our sources. Were you acquainted with the deceased, Carol Olsen?"

The mere mention of the name triggers a fresh set of sobs. Between the choking and gasping, she fits her reply. "We were friends in primary school. She was from Québec, too."

Erick nods, and I stare at my mood ring, hoping for a bolt of inspiration.

No such luck.

"And when was the last time you saw Carol Olsen?"

An over-the-top wail, and both hands cover her face.

Rolling my eyes, I exhale. She smells about as guilty as they come. This false remorse isn't fooling anyone. I hope.

"Miss Tremblay, I need you to answer these questions truthfully. You're a suspect in a homicide. If ballistics match your gun to the bullet recovered from the scene—"

"NO!" Carol Tremblay screams from the back-seat. "No! I would never hurt her. You don't under-stand. I have a gun for protection. That's all."

Erick takes the outburst in stride. "And what do you need protection from, Miss Tremblay?"

Her soft French accent utters a phrase that shocks both Erick and me. "My father is Antoine Bergeron. If you know anything about the maple syrup mafia, you're familiar with the name. He sent me to the states for college, but by the time I finished, his notoriety was catching up with him. He didn't think it was safe for me to return to Canada, so he arranged for me to emigrate."

My eyes are wide as saucers. My psychic senses must've known about the connection, even though it hadn't bubbled to my consciousness. "So when I used that name—"

Her breath shudders. "Exactly. Edith didn't tell me your full name until you rushed off so suddenly, but, as soon as she did, I grabbed my pocketbook and ran. I had no way of knowing if it was a message from my father, or a threat. It certainly couldn't have been a coincidence. My first thought was to get to my father and find out what I was supposed to do. If someone was trying to kill me, I thought he would be my best protection."

Erick's hands grip the steering wheel, twisting forward and back as though he's working the throttle on a motorcycle. "What does any of this have to do with Carol Olsen? Did she find out you were having an affair with her father-in-law?"

Miss Tremblay lays her head back and gazes up at the ceiling of the cruiser. "I suppose it's all going to come out now. She and I kept each other's secrets for so long . . . I never thought it would come to this."

He squares his shoulders. "Well, it has come to this. Tell me the nature of the relationship between you and Mrs. Olsen, and tell me the truth about the last time you saw her."

Miss Tremblay wrings her hands, swipes the tears from her cheeks, and inhales a shaky breath. "Carol and I were involved. It's why she left Wayne."

Turning my head to the side, I glance at Erick and silently mouth, "What?"

He ignores my pantomime. "Please continue, Miss Tremblay."

"My father sent me enough money each month to get by, but Carol was always the dreamer. She wanted more. She wanted us to be ridiculously wealthy. So she refused to divorce Wayne, because she knew he would inherit the cranberry farm someday, and thought that would be our ticket. I had my doubts. Working alongside Niklas every day didn't give me much hope in the inheritance scheme. He was healthy as an ox, and none too fond of his wife. Most days he spent twelve hours at the farm. Occasionally he even slept in his office."

"Go on."

"I wanted to make Carol happy, and thought I could speed things up with a blackmail scheme. I befriended him, brought him coffee and lingered in his office, and occasionally ordered dinner for the two of us. Honestly, when I got to know him, I really disliked the blackmail idea. So I dragged my feet."

The whistle on my teakettle can only be silent for so long. "For ten years?"

"Yes. I know it sounds ridiculous, but I didn't want to sleep with him. He's not my type, you know?" Her voice cracks a little, and my heart hurts for her loss.

Erick gestures for her to continue.

"I kept coming up with excuses every time Carol pushed for blackmail photos. Besides, she kept working a variety of her own scams. But when she dove into the maple syrup trade, I was afraid. I knew how dangerous it could be, and I thought I'd pull the extortion trigger and save us both."

My arm is cramping and I have to adjust the angle I'm holding the recording device.

"It wasn't difficult to coax Niklas to a hotel. Carol hid in the closet and took some compromising photos. I didn't even actually have to sleep with him. I offered to give him a massage, and, during the rubdown, he fell asleep. The photos told a different story, and we were sure we could get him to pay."

Erick nods. "What happened when you gave him the photos?"

Carol Tremblay groans and hangs her head. "That was the day Norma visited the office."

Sheriff Harper presses her. "Did Norma Olsen come into the office often?"

"*Absolument pas.* I mean, absolutely not. In all the years I'd worked there, I'd only seen her three times. Including that day. Niklas was out inspecting one of the cranberry bogs for dewberry invasion, and she insisted on waiting in his office. I was sitting at my desk sweating profusely. The corner of the envelope was sticking out from under the blotter on his desk. As the minutes ticked away, Mrs. Olsen got antsy. She started poking around, and she found the pictures."

Once again, my pressure valve releases. "Did she confront you? Did you run?"

Miss Tremblay shrugs. "The angle of the photos never showed the face of the woman. Carol and I planned it that way. But once I saw her pull out the envelope, I wasn't going to stick around to find out. I grabbed my purse and ran to my car. I called Niklas to tell him his wife was waiting in his office and she looked angry. He hung up on me."

I turn toward the backseat. "Was he upset about the incident in the hotel room?"

My mouth is running, and Erick's stern gaze reminds me I'm supposed to be seen and not heard.

"Not likely. He just didn't like to be disturbed when he was in the bogs."

Sheriff Harper leaps back into the fray. "So what happened when Niklas talked to his wife?"

Carol Tremblay sighs and shakes her pretty blonde head. "She insisted he retire, effective immediately. He negotiated for two weeks' transition and leaned heavily on Wayne."

"So Wayne Olsen knew about the retirement for two weeks?" My face scrunches with concern.

She hems and haws. "Not exactly. Niklas didn't want anyone to know he was retiring. He was insistent that Wayne come in and learn more about the business, but it wasn't until last Friday night at the actual retirement party that Wayne discovered when he'd be taking everything over—when business reopens after the holiday break."

A relieved sigh escapes Erick's lips, and he stares off into the distance. I can't be sure whether he's collecting his thoughts, or if he's lost his train of thought. Luckily, I'm happy to jump in.

"Now for the part you keep avoiding. When was the last time you saw Carol Olsen—alive?" I move the recorder toward the metal divider.

She swallows hard, looks at the recorder, and briefly glances at me. "In the woods, behind that Twiggy woman's cabin."

Erick is back online. "And what were you doing in the woods behind Twiggy's cabin?"

"Once I admitted how the blackmail scheme

had failed, Carol wanted me to seduce her husband. I told her I couldn't do it. I told her I didn't want to do it. So she came up with the crazy notion of getting pictures of Wayne and Twiggy, and using them to blackmail Wayne into buying her out of Crimson Crest. Since they were technically still married, you know,"

"Solid plan."

Erick darts a scornful gaze in my direction. "Moon, let's keep it professional."

"Copy that."

"While we were sneaking around in the woods trying to decide the best vantage point to get photos, a shot rang out."

The sheriff's head drops forward. "Miss Tremblay, do you expect me to believe that you and the deceased randomly had an idea, known only to the two of you, and yet a killer managed to find you and kill Carol Olsen. Could you please explain to me why someone would want to kill Mrs. Olsen?"

Carol Tremblay seems to shrink in the backseat, and she hugs her arms tightly around her stomach as she hunches forward and whispers, "She was wearing my coat."

My eyes are brimming with unshed tears and I seek out Erick's. He nods toward the phone and I end the recording.

CHAPTER 17

AN UNEASY SILENCE stifles all conversation inside the cruiser. My extrasensory perception confirms Carol Tremblay is telling the truth, and clearly in mourning.

Erick's jaw is tight, and his hands grip the steering wheel even more fiercely. It doesn't take a psychic to figure out what he's thinking.

Carol Olsen wasn't the target. She was a victim of mistaken identity. Carol Tremblay was not the murderer, she was the intended victim. And last, but not least by any means, the murderer is still at large.

Time for me to focus. Put all my special gifts to use and come up with something that will close this case and save a woman's life. Miss Tremblay is heartbroken. She lost her life partner, but, even worse, the survivor's guilt is crushing her. I'm sure she can't help but wonder what would've happened if she'd worn her own coat that day.

Don't worry, I'm not going soft on Carol Olsen. She seemed like a real piece of work. She clearly put Wayne through the wringer more than once and was willing to do just about anything to make a buck. I'm not saying the world will be worse off without her, but my heart goes out to those she left behind.

Sinking into myself, I twist the mood ring on my left hand and work hard to clear my mind of distracting thoughts.

Feelings of anger and revenge tighten my chest as the word *vendetta* pops into my head. Simultaneously, my mood ring burns, and I glance down to see maple syrup spilling from a large steel drum. Looks like the kind of drums they transport crude oil in, but I'm no expert.

"Miss Tremblay?"

Her breath is ragged, but she replies. "Yes."

"I have a hunch they targeted you because your father double-crossed someone. Would he have any reason to dispose of perfectly good maple syrup?"

Carol gasps and presses a hand to her chest. "How could you—?"

Erick looks at me and arches one eyebrow.

"I think it has something to do with that. Do you know if he has any partners, or—"

"I don't know if he's done it lately—we've been out of touch for several years—but I remember one time he forced exporters to buy from him, by sabotaging their inventory. I don't know exactly what that meant, but he may have poured it out."

"How long ago was that?"

"At least five years ago. But my father has a lot of enemies. He's an unscrupulous businessman who won't take no for an answer. If he did it once, it's possible he did it again—more recently."

Erick looks at me and scrunches up his face in confusion.

With my hand below seat level, so Miss Tremblay can't see, I give him the gesture to simmer down. "Carol, you're going to be in danger until we catch the person who murdered Mrs. Olsen. It seems to me you were the intended target. Once word gets out that it wasn't you wearing that jacket, I'm sure the killer will try again. Would you be willing to help us catch him or her?"

She sniffles and asks for a tissue.

Erick retrieves a tissue box from under the driver's seat. I push one through the metal grating and wait while she blows her nose and wipes her tears. "If it means we can catch the person who murdered her, I'll do whatever you ask."

"Would you be willing to lie to your father?" I chew the inside of my cheek while I wait for her reply. I know it's a big ask, but if she's as estranged from her father as it sounds, I'm hoping her loyalty to Carol Olsen will win out.

"Maybe. What did you have in mind?"

"Let's assume that the assassin was either a rival, or was hired by a rival. I want to call your father with a ransom demand, and then I'll put you on the phone and you'll need to act terrified."

Her breathing comes in shallow gasps and she shakes her head. "I don't know. I don't know if I can do this."

"If he's recently double-crossed someone, he may say their name or give us some other clue that would lead us to the killer. I know it's a gamble, but if it pays off, it means— It means she didn't die in vain."

Carol Tremblay tucks her blonde hair behind her ears and presses a hand over her mouth as she considers my plan. "All right. I'll do it."

Erick looks at me and shakes his head.

"I'm not asking you to participate, Erick. But you know I'm right. If Antoine Bergeron gives us a clue to the killer's identity, we'll have a much better chance of protecting her."

He eases the squad car to the side of the road

and turns off the engine. "We're not doing this at the station."

"Copy that. Can you hand me her phone?"

Erick rifles through the box of bagged evidence and pulls out a clear plastic bag holding her phone. "Put on a pair of gloves."

Nodding my head, I pick up the gloves he's pointing to, put them on, and carefully remove the phone from the evidence bag.

After I join Carol Tremblay in the backseat, we go over the plan one more time.

"Pardon, but you left the door open. It's getting awfully cold in here. Can you close it?"

"It will be more realistic if you're shivering. I'm going to leave it open, all right?"

She nods, takes the phone, and places the call.

"Put it on speaker. And let me talk first."

A deep voice with a thick French accent pours from the speaker. "Chère fille? Is it you?"

I loosen my throat to lower my voice an octave and lean into my gruffer tones. "I'll ask the questions, Bergeron."

"Who is this? What have you done with my daughter? If you harm a hair on her head—"

"What will you do? Pour out some more of my Canadian gold?" I'm spitballing here, but hopefully I'm on the right track.

"Olsen? Are you working with the old man

now? It's not enough that you attempted to steal the contracts of my exporters, now you're in league with Leblanc?"

"You didn't think we'd let you get away with it, did you?"

"I poured out a few barrels to teach you a lesson. This isn't worth the life of my daughter! What do you want from me?"

I look at Carol and shrug. She mouths to me, "All the sugar makers."

"I want first crack at all the sugar makers, Bergeron. You get out of my way, or you'll never see your daughter alive again."

He moans, and there's a loud thumping on his end of the phone. Possibly his fist hitting the table. "How do I know you haven't already harmed her? Put her on the phone."

Glancing at Carol, I arch an eyebrow and lift my shoulders.

She nods and reaches for the phone.

My plan to leave the door open has worked marvelously. Her teeth are chattering in earnest. Her voice is broken and filled with fear as she speaks to her father. "Papa? Papa, they mean to kill me."

"Put Olsen back on the phone." His tone is all business now.

Interesting that he thinks I'm Carol Olsen. He

clearly hasn't heard about the murder that took place south of the Canadian border. However, that luck won't hold out long. We need to get some details to flush out Leblanc. "You're to meet Leblanc at the usual place with one million in US currency. You have twelve hours."

"What? One million? US?" He growls, and the sound of shattering glass tinkles down the line. "It will take me at least two days to get the money and fly out to Pin Cherry. Ask Leblanc for more time."

Erick waves a hand to get my attention and drags a finger across his neck. I end the call, and we all breathe a sigh of relief. "Is that enough?"

Erick shrugs. "Let's hope. Turn the phone off in case he tries to call back. You did a good job, Miss Tremblay. Hop up front, Mitzy. I've got to call Paulsen."

Before exiting the backseat, I can't stop myself from giving Carol Tremblay a comforting hug. I know what it's like to lose someone you care about. She squeezes my hand and thanks me.

Sheriff Harper eases the cruiser back onto the road as he calls dispatch.

"Dispatch, Sheriff Harper here. Send Paulsen and Johnson to pick up Niklas Olsen."

"Bring him to the station?"

"10-4. Hold him for questioning."

Even with my special gifts, I can't see where

Erick's logic is headed. "Why are you bringing in Niklas? Shouldn't we be calling CC to ask him to pick up this Leblanc character?"

Erick shakes his head, and his eyes are stormy. "You heard what Bergeron said, 'Are you working with the old man now?' and when you mentioned the usual meeting place, he immediately assumed Pin Cherry. Also, Leblanc—"

"Means The White! The old man with the white hair is Niklas Olsen. But that means—"

Carol Tremblay sobs from the back. "That means he tried to kill me in retaliation for the blackmail, and he was secretly running illegal maple syrup behind everyone's back."

My wheels are spinning out of control now, and I'm certain there's actual smoke pouring from my ears. "He must've employed you to have leverage over your father. How do you think he knew you were Bergeron's daughter?"

"Maybe Carol mentioned that we were old school chums when she recommended me for the job. I'm certain I never mentioned it. I'm always quite careful."

My hand shoots across the car and I grip Erick's arm. "What if he meant to kill his daughter-in-law? A coat might confuse a hired gun, but Niklas would know the difference."

Erick nods thoughtfully. "But his illness . . . He can barely walk."

My mouth blurts before my brain engages. "I could grab his medical records if—"

"Absolutely not. We can subpoena records, Miss Moon."

"Of course. Whatever you say, Sheriff." Sufficiently scolded, I fold my hands in my lap and sit quietly for the rest of the ride.

CHAPTER 18

ERICK LEAVES me to fend for myself as he escorts Carol Tremblay into the station. It's unclear whether she's here as an actual suspect, or if completing her interview is simply a matter of proper paperwork.

I stop at the front desk and clear my plan with Furious Monkeys. "Is it all right if I head back?"

She chuckles. "Isn't it always?"

Fair play to the gamer. Pushing through the swinging gate, I'm forced to stop in the bullpen when a scuffle in the hallway alerts me to Deputy Paulsen bringing Niklas Olsen toward Interrogation Room 1.

They picked him up quickly. I better grab a front-row seat in the observation room and see if this old fella has any tricks up his sleeve.

As soon as Paulsen leads him into the interrogation room, I rush down the hallway and dive into the room sandwiched between the two interrogation bays and flanked with wide one-way glass.

Erick is finishing up with Carol Tremblay in Interrogation Room 2. He has her recorded statement, but she's making some notes about dates and times, and her unsavory family connections. She signs the paper and pushes it across the table.

"Sheriff Harper, when may I collect Carol's body? I'd like to plan a proper memorial service, you know, before they move her into storage until the spring thaw." Miss Tremblay stumbles over her words, and fresh tears spring to the corners of her eyes.

Erick inhales sharply. "I'm sorry, Miss Tremblay, but Carol Olsen is technically still married to Wayne Olsen. He's the only person who can make arrangements for her remains."

Miss Tremblay's bottom lip quivers and she shakes her head. "That won't do. That just won't do."

He slides his chair back, gets to his feet, and places a comforting hand on her shoulder. "I'll talk to Wayne. He's a reasonable man."

The daughter of the northern hemisphere's most notorious maple syrup Mafioso gazes up at Erick as though he's personally promised to fly her to the pearly gates. "Would you? Oh, I'm so— Thank you. You have no idea what this means to me. Thank you." She clutches his hand with both of hers and squeezes tightly as tears trickle down her cheeks.

Sheriff Harper drags his hand away and exits the cubicle of uncomfortable emotions.

Clicking the room two speaker off, I rotate my attention toward room one and click the silver toggle.

Erick enters with a thick manila folder in his hands. He doesn't greet Niklas. Instead, he pulls out his chair, deliberately lowers himself into it, and drops the thick file onto the table with a thud. "Seems like you weren't completely honest with us the last time you were here, Mr. Olsen."

Niklas no longer appears the doddering, aged retiree. He lounges in the stiff steel chair as though born to it. His eyes glint with resistance, and he makes no response.

"Deputy Johnson has notified you of your Miranda rights, is that correct?"

Niklas nods once.

"Mr. Olsen, you'll have to reply verbally for the recording. Have you been advised of your Miranda rights?"

He offers an audible, "Yes." Followed by a silent sneer.

This is an absolute Dr. Jekyll and Mr. Hyde moment. The friendly, helpful gentlemen who suffered from a debilitating illness and retired at his wife's request has vanished. The man that sits across from the sheriff is cagey and defiant. I wouldn't trust him as far as I could throw him. And if you remember anything about my athletic ability, I can't even throw a ball decently.

"Mr. Olsen, is it true that you are involved in illegal maple syrup trade with several sugar makers in Québec?"

Niklas does not answer.

"Mr. Olsen, I have transcriptions of phone calls, copies of email messages, and copies of text messages between you and four of the most well-known maple rebels. You've been under surveillance by the Canadian Mounties for some time."

There's a distinct shift in Niklas Olsen's energy. He was confident he'd managed to stay under the radar of the authorities in the United States, but it clearly had not occurred to him that some of his contacts on the Canadian side of the border might be huge blips on the Mounties' radar.

"Do you know of any connection between your executive secretary Carol Tremblay and the Canadian businessman known as Antoine Bergeron?"

Niklas makes every effort to remain stoic, but my psychic senses pickup on a surge of fear and loathing. The name means something to him, and he absolutely knew about the connection.

Erick ignores the lack of response and moves on. "What did you do when your wife confronted you regarding the affair and the compromising photos taken of you and Miss Tremblay at a motel in Broken Rock?"

The crispy exterior of Mr. Olsen finally cracks. "There was no affair."

The sheriff removes several racy photos from the folder and pushes them across the table toward Mr. Olsen. "These photos tell a different story."

The muscles in the accused man's jaw clench twice. "That's what her father thought, too."

Pump the brakes! Plot twist. He used the black-mail photos that the Carols took of him to blackmail them? I shouldn't be rubbing my hands together so eagerly, but this turn of events fascinates me.

"So you were aware of Miss Tremblay's true identity and family connections."

"That's the only reason I hired her."

The phrase is so cold and calculating, my skin crawls like that of a shedding snake.

"So why would you attempt to blackmail Miss Tremblay?"

"I wasn't. I used the photos to manipulate her father to hand over some contracts. The cranberry business ain't what it used to be, Harper. Wayne doesn't want anything to do with it. Norma couldn't manage her way out of a paper sack. I could've sold the whole operation to one of those big conglomerates ten or fifteen years ago. But I thought my legacy meant something to my son. Boy, was I mistaken. Now that they've bought up all the mom-and-pop bogs, nobody is interested. I was out of options and I had to take care of my family. Had to provide for my retirement."

Erick shuffles papers and gazes directly at Mr. Olsen. "And by providing for your retirement, you mean illegally importing maple syrup, stockpiling it to drive up the price, and selling it at your convenience to the highest bidder?"

Niklas practically spits his reply. "That about sums it up."

Well, Erick definitely has him on the illegal importing, but I'm still not completely convinced this man murdered his daughter-in-law.

"Mr. Olsen, where were you Saturday evening between 8:00 p.m. and midnight?"

Niklas lifts his chin defiantly and crosses his arms. "You already seem to have all the answers, Harper. Why don't you tell me?"

"Very well. It is the belief of this department that you were trespassing on Susan Matthews' property—"

"Who's Susan Matthews?" Niklas tilts his head.

"You probably know her as Twiggy."

My jaw hits the floor faster than a drunk at happy hour. Twiggy's actual name isn't Twiggy? Did I know that? My entire world is turning upside down. Twiggy is Susan Matthews. I hope to never hear that name again. It doesn't fit.

Shoot, my existential crisis stole my attention from the interrogation. Erick is mid-sentence when I regain my focus.

". . . carrying a 308 hunting rifle with a silencer, and you shot your daughter-in-law, Carol Olsen. You did not seek medical assistance for her, but instead left her in the snow to die of her wound. That sounds like homicide in the first degree, Mr. Olsen. What do you have to say for yourself?"

The jutted chin drops, but his anger continues to rise. "She made a fool of my son—of my whole family. She was never interested in Wayne. Carol was not that kind of girl, if you know what I mean. She married him to try to get her hands on the family money. When she found out he didn't want to take over the Crimson Crest, she hightailed it out of their house and looked for another scam. She was always conning someone. I'm not convinced she even had feelings for this Carol Tremblay. I think it was just another one of her long cons." His hand smacks onto the table with enough force to make the whole surface tremble. "It may not have been right to take a life, but the world isn't going to be any worse off for the lack of Carol Olsen."

My extrasensory perception gets a jolt of anticipation emanating from Erick. However, on that side of the glass, he maintains his cool. "Mr. Olsen, are you saying you shot and killed Carol Olsen?"

The ire seems to have run its course, and his arms drop to his sides as his head dips. "I didn't mean to kill her. I wanted to scare them. She found out about my maple syrup deals and she was trying to worm her way into that. I was sick and tired of all her wheeling and dealing. Only meant to wing her, but my eyesight isn't what it used to be."

Erick's shoulders rise and fall as he takes a single calming breath. "Mr. Olsen, did you shoot Carol Olsen in the woods Saturday evening?"

The elderly man's eyelids rise and he meets Erick's gaze. "Yes. I shot Carol. But I didn't mean to kill her."

The hasty addition of his closing phrase seems more like a plan to mount his own defense than an accurate statement. If you ask me, he was tired of Carol Olsen messing around with his family, and he put an end to it the only way he knew how. And if it happened to hurt the secretary who tried to blackmail him in the process, seems like that was a bonus he didn't mind.

Erick removes handcuffs from his duty belt and

approaches Mr. Olsen. "Niklas Olsen, I am placing you under arrest on suspicion of the murder of Carol Olsen." He slips the handcuffs around the man's wrists and walks him out of Interrogation Room 1.

For the record, Mr. Olsen needed neither cane, walker, nor wheelchair for this journey. His medical condition seems as phony as his original alibi. When I place my hand on the doorknob, it twists on its own. Stepping back, I'm pleased to see Erick entering, and not deputy Paulsen.

"How did you get all those transcripts and stuff so quickly?"

He blushes. "It was ninety-five percent blank pages. I had some notes on the top, and a couple photos—"

My voice escapes me for a minute as I stare in awe. "You were bluffing?"

His voice is thick with emotion. "I learned from the best."

As I formulate my comeback—

He pushes the door closed behind him and pulls me into an unexpected embrace.

"To what do I owe this pleasure, Sheriff Harper?"

His hands slide down the curve of my back as tingles rise along my spine. "I just need to wrap my arms around something I can trust. I know my line of work shows me a window into the darker side of humanity, but some families are really messed up."

I snake my arms around his neck and gaze up into his beautiful blue eyes. "Lucky for us, we're totally normal."

My obvious joke does the trick, and he laughs softly as he presses his lips to mine. "So Christmas Eve supper at your dad's house tomorrow, right?"

"That's right, *boyfriend*. You're going to be front and center with all the Duncan-Moon—"

My conversation with Isadora floods into my head and interrupts my flow. The word family holds a different meaning for me now.

Erick brushes my snow-white hair back from my forehead. "What's wrong? I don't like that look. Is there something going on between you and your dad?"

Letting my arms fall away from his broad shoulders, I step back. "I have to take care of something. And I can't talk about it right now. Is it still all right if I come over to your place tonight, after I handle my business?"

Concern creates two lines between his eyebrows as he tilts his head. "You're not going to put yourself in any danger, are you?"

"Rude."

He lifts his hands in surrender and chuckles. "Come on, I have to ask."

"Fair enough. No. I will not be in any physical danger. It's more of an emotional minefield than anything else."

"Okay. I'll pick something up at the diner once I finish up my paperwork, and see you at my place, whenever you get there."

Pushing up on my tiptoes, I kiss his soft, full lips, squeeze my arms around him, and wish I never had to let go.

He's the first to extract himself this time. "Hey, save some of that initiative for later."

My cheeks flush pin-cherry red and he exits the room ahead of me.

Deputy Paulsen is dead center in the bullpen when I attempt to make my escape. "Hey, Moon."

Blerg. The last thing I need in my current fragile emotional state is a confrontation with Pauly Paulsen. "I was just leaving."

"You give Twiggy a message for me, eh?"

"I suppose. What's the message?" My arms are crossed, and my hip may be kicked out in a some-what defiant pose.

Paulsen steps closer and lowers her voice. "You tell her I never thought she was guilty for a minute. Got that?"

The unexpected kind words from the bully-esque deputy, and the blind faith in my cantan-kerous employee, catch me off guard. Before I know what's happening, I throw my arms around Deputy Paulsen's shoulders and I'm hugging her tightly as she sputters. "Easy, Moon. Our entire department isn't up for grabs, you know."

I release her stout, stubborn form and chuckle as I sashay through the hanging wooden gate. I don't think I've ever seen her blush. Let's call that a win.

Outside the station, I plant my feet perpendicular to the street and my heart is torn in two directions. I could call Silas and drag this out, but I know what I have to do, and there's no point in chickening out or delaying the inevitable. Rather than head back to the bookshop, I steel my nerves and step into the diner.

Odell offers me the standard spatula salute through the red-Formica trimmed orders-up window.

The waterworks threaten to unleash. Swallowing hard, I inhale through my nose and exhale through my mouth—just as every yoga instructor in Sedona recommends—before marching into the kitchen.

"What's up, Mitzy? You here to eat or just chew the fat?"

"How would you feel about closing early today, Odell?"

He glances out the orders-up window at the

empty restaurant and shrugs. "I could be convinced. Whaddya got in mind?"

The tears are creeping to the edge of my eyelids now, and I think I only have room for one more sentence. "Can you just close, and come with me?"

The man has always been quick on the uptake. He looks at my face, removes his apron, and walks out to lock the front door.

He flips the sign from open to closed and leads the way to the back door. I slip my arm through his elbow, and we make our way down Main Street toward First Avenue and my bookshop.

I honestly wonder if I'm doing the right thing.

CHAPTER 19

THE BOOKSHOP and its secrets get closer with each step.

Odell must sense my unease. "What's goin' on, kid? You got something nasty clogging the pipes in your apartment?"

The leftfield query catches me off guard and laughter comes too soon and too loud. "Oh my gosh, it's nothing like that. But thanks for breaking the ice."

He runs a hand through his short grey buzz cut and shakes his head. "Breaking the ice? I thought I was practically family." His laughter is rough as a Brillo pad and comforting as a favorite shirt.

It's funny that he would mention family. He's more family than he knows. "I don't want to spoil the surprise."

"Well, I hope you didn't get me a present. Because I didn't get you one, and I don't plan on running out to the stores at this late date." He shoves a hand in the pocket of his dungarees.

Classic Odell. Practical, down-to-earth, honest. I hope those traits pull him through what I'm about to reveal.

We tramp across the street in the icy slush, and he pauses in typical Odell fashion. "Front door or side door?"

"Let's go in the front door. That feels right to me."

He shrugs his shoulders and waits while I fish out my key and unlock my beautiful door.

Stepping inside the darkened interior, our only guiding illumination is the light leaking through the windows from the streetlamp on the corner.

"Wait here." I race to the back room and flip the lights on. I remember the first time I walked into this place and hopelessly searched the walls by the front door for a switch. The indomitable Twiggy blew past me and solved my problem. Just another of the sweet memories I have of falling in love with this town and its people. I sure hope what I'm about to do doesn't ruin all that.

As I walk back, Odell meets me at the bottom of the circular staircase. I unhook the "No Admittance" chain and offer a warning. "Hurry. I gotta hook it back up in thirty seconds—or else."

He hustles up a few treads and waits for me. "No one wants to draw Twiggy's wrath, eh?"

The fresh incident of Twiggy landing on a suspect list, paired with Odell's comment, makes me giggle nervously. I hook up the chain and motion for him to continue.

He walks into the Rare Books Loft, pauses and turns a full three hundred and sixty degrees. "Boy, this place is gorgeous. Doesn't matter how many times I take a gander, each time is as sweet as the first. Did ya bring me up here to show me some books?"

I can sense his tension building, and I have to assume the last time he was in the apartment was when my grandmother was still alive. I smile, and push past him to pull the candle handle next to my copy of *Saducismus Triumphatus* and silently watch as the bookcase door slides open. "Come on in and have a seat. Like I said, I have a surprise for you."

He hesitates a moment, but walks forward like the brave soldier he is. Odell pauses next to the seating arrangement and chooses the settee. As he perches on the edge with obvious discomfort, Grams blasts out of the closet in mid-sentence.

"Finally! I have so many outfit—"

The sight of her makes me doubt my decision. Am I doing this? Yeah. All right, I'm doing this.

Isadora whizzes toward me at ludicrous speed. "Are you doing what? You better not be doing what I think you're doing, young lady!"

"Odell. I know this is going to sound crazy, and I won't blame you if you get up and run out of here, but Grams isn't as dearly departed as everyone thinks."

His brown eyes search my face for any hint of amusement. Finding none, he gets to his feet. "What are you saying, Mitzy?"

Here goes nothing, or maybe everything. "Silas and Grams figured out a way to tether her spirit to this bookshop. And I can see ghosts. So, I can see her and talk to her, and she has something very important to tell you."

He sinks back to the settee with an unreadable gaze.

I'm unsure if it's disbelief, shock, or dread. "Odell? Did you hear what I said?"

He grips his knees with weathered hands, and I can see his knuckles whiten as he struggles to steady himself. "I'm old, but my ears still work."

Uh oh. That sounds anger adjacent.

Isadora floats toward him like a cloud on a gentle breeze. "Of course he's angry, Mitzy. You should've talked to me about this. This is a terrible idea."

She's so busy scolding me, she doesn't realize how close she's come to Odell. But I immediately recognize the ghost-chill bumps rising on his arms.

His eyes widen and he looks at me. "Is it cold in here?"

"It's Isadora. She's here."

His face softens as hope fills the lines around his eyes. He braves a smile. "Myrtle, is that you?"

She swirls closer and another chill grips him.

"Well, if this is what you got me for Christmas, Mitzy, I know I can't top it."

Tears spill from the corners of my eyes, and I join him on the settee. "There's actually— I hate to be the one to— No. I take that back. I'm actually ecstatic to be the one to tell you this. And I'm sorry you're only finding out now. Although, speaking from experience, later is better than never."

His eyes are misty, and I feel like he's holding his breath.

"In a couple minutes, I'm going to leave. That stack of 3 x 5 cards on the coffee table is how she can communicate with you. She can write you messages or whatever. You can ask her anything you want. Make sense?"

He nods mutely.

"But before I go, I'm going to tell you this part

because, well, honestly, I don't entirely trust her to tell you herself."

Grams rests a bejeweled fist on her hip. "Well, I never!"

Without thinking, I toss back my usual response. "We all know that's not true, Myrtle Isadora Johnson Linder Duncan Willamet Rogers."

Odell chuckles. "You're startin' to make a believer out of me."

Swiping at a tear, I push onward. "Now, I hope you think this is wonderful news. I think it's wonderful news, and—"

He takes my hand and gently pats it. "Just say it, kid. The longer you wait, the harder it gets. Trust me, I learned that the hard way." His gaze drifts off, and I'm certain he's referring to keeping his true feelings about my grandmother hidden for so many decades.

"All right. You're my grandfather."

He smiles pleasantly, nods, and pats my hand again. "Of course. I'll always be your stand-in grandfather. What does that have to do with your news?"

"What I mean is, you can drop the stand-in. You're Jacob's father. You're my biological grandfather."

Isadora rockets toward the ceiling and her quiet sobs drift down like ghost rain.

Odell sits stock-still. Like a deer caught in the headlights or a jackrabbit listening to the approach of a predator from above.

"Please say something." I turn toward him, filled with worry and anticipation.

He chews the inside of his cheek, works his lips back and forth, and exhales.

My heart is thundering in my chest and I can't keep quiet. "I'm excited about this news. It's weird, and I don't know how my dad's gonna react, but I'm on board. I'm all for it. I want you to come to our Christmas Eve supper tomorrow night as my grandfather. Will you come?"

Odell's eyes darken and his voice is barely audible. "She's here, right?"

"That's right. She's up there, by the window. Do you want to ask her something?"

"Myrtle, we need to talk."

She flutters toward the 3 x 5 cards and picks up the pen.

His sharp intake of breath indicates any lingering doubts have vanished.

"All right. I'm gonna run next door and bring my dad up to speed. Unless you want to tell Jacob yourself?"

He shakes his head. "You do whatever you think is best. I'm gonna need some time, kid. You just gave me a drink from a firehose."

Nodding, I get to my feet and put on my coat. "Grams, I expect you to be absolutely honest with Odell. There's nothing to hide. No more secrets. Promise?"

She clutches her pearls, and I can sense her struggling with her reply. "I'll do it, sweetie. I promise."

As I head toward the door to take my leave, Pyewacket crawls out from underneath the bed, saunters across the room, and curls up next to Odell on the settee.

"I leave you in good paws, Odell. I'm hanging out with Erick tonight, so stay as long as you like. Grams will show you how to set the main alarm when you leave. And, I hope we'll see you at supper tomorrow night."

He presses his lips together tightly, but offers no reply.

Pushing the twisted ivy medallion, I wait for the door to slide open and step into the Rare Books Loft with a wistful grin.

My dad keeps insisting we build a Frida Kahlo/Diego Rivera walkway between the third floors of our buildings, but I'm not sure I'm *that* comfortable with living next door to him. I mean, I already have to deal with the constant ghost-trusions of Grams. I don't need my mama-bear of a dad interrupting my alone time with my beau. However, Jacob and I exchanged keys not long after he remodeled the building across the alley from my bookshop. So, I let myself into the Restorative Justice Foundation and take the elevator up to the penthouse suite.

Three sets of eyes spin from the supper table when the bells pings and the doors slide open.

Amaryllis is the first to react. "Mitzy! You're just in time. I was testing out some recipes for Christmas Eve supper, and I have an absolute mountain of garlic-mashed potatoes. Can I fix you a plate?"

My brain says no, but my stomach growls loudly.

My smart aleck stepbrother apparently has the hearing of a canine. "That sounded like a yes from your belly."

Rolling my eyes, I approach the table and take the empty chair next to my dad.

The spread laid out smells wonderful, and my brain finally catches up with my stomach. I am extremely hungry. Amaryllis is an even better cook than she is a lawyer.

A moment later, she places a plate in front of me, piled high with mashed potatoes, roasted root vegetables, and a juicy slice of prime rib.

"This looks amazing! Are we having prime rib for Christmas dinner?"

She sits down, lays her napkin and across her lap, and winks. "No. But pretending we were, so I could make a *practice* recipe, was the only way to get your father to drive to Grand Falls and pick one up for me."

Jacob smiles and they share an adorable chuckle.

"So, I guess the honeymoon is still going strong over here, eh?"

Stellen guffaws and quickly covers his mouth with a napkin.

Amaryllis blushes. "Are we really that bad?"

Stellen takes a long pull of his sparkling apple cider and smiles. "You guys are adorable. I can only hope I have the chance to be as in love as you two. Although, I gotta say, I'm pleased to be away at college."

Warm laughter fills the room, and, if not for the potential dark cloud of my news, I would feel as happy as ever.

It's almost been a year since my father married this amazing woman, and they adopted Stellen. I want to believe these people are the kind who value choosing a family, and will welcome Odell with open arms, but who can predict—

Right, the psychic. Sure would be nice if my mood ring would give me some indication of which way this news is going to land.

To be clear, the ring does nothing.

Tales of successful rehabilitants in the Restorative Justice program, hilarious college anecdotes, and even a couple Pyewacket stories occupy the rest of our supper conversation.

At the end of the meal, Stellen offers to help Amaryllis clear up, and I put a hand on my father's arm. "Can we talk? In private."

He leans close and whispers, "If Sheriff Harper knocked you up, I'll have more than a word with him."

The thought nearly chokes me, and I pound an open hand on my chest in an attempt to catch my breath. "Don't even joke about that, Dad. Do not."

His grey eyes twinkle with mischief, and a broad smile sweeps across his face. "I don't know. Would it be so bad?"

"Dad!" I punch him playfully on the shoulder.

He pushes his chair back and beckons me to follow. There's a small study between the kitchen and the hallway leading to the bedrooms. We step inside and he grips the edge of the door. "Door closed or open?"

"Closed, for now."

We share the cinnamon-brown leather sofa, and he offers me a throw blanket.

"I'm all right. Eating always warms me up."

"What's on your mind, sweetie?"

"Grams and I had a bit of a tiff, and I forced her to spill some secrets she'd hoped to take to the grave. At first I wasn't sure if I had a right to tell anyone, but I've learned the hard way that keeping secrets rarely pays off."

He nods. "Your grandmother passed away a few years ago. Are you sure this secret even needs to come out?"

"Yeah, I think it does. Because it affects people who are still alive."

His spine stiffens, and I sense that edge he earned in prison warning him of imminent danger.

"It's not bad. At least I don't think it's bad. It's just—"

"Just say it, sweetie. The longer you wait, the harder it gets."

The déjà vu of that phrase is uncanny. Here I go using that word uncanny again. "You're right. I'm just gonna rip off the bandage."

He takes my hand and looks at me with all a father's love. "I'm ready."

"Cal wasn't your biological father."

Jacob's large hand slackens its grip on mine and there's cold sweat in his palm. "What? But they were married. I was a month premature, but—"

His eyes widen as several pieces of his child-hood mythos crumble before him.

"Grams didn't know she was pregnant when

she married Cal. She found out right after their quickie nuptials and decided to bury the truth. From the minute she told him she was expecting, everyone believed the child was his."

Jacob sighs heavily. "So, my real— No, I don't want to say that. Cal was my real father. The biological father, or sperm donor, was someone she met in rehab?"

My dad is understandably angry, and I'm hoping the truth will be a welcome relief.

"It's Odell. Odell Johnson is your father."

He hunches forward and drops his face into his hands.

I place a comforting hand on his back and rub little circles. "I know it's a lot, Dad. But I'd be lying if I said I wasn't excited. My grandfather is alive. Your dad is alive." Images of the moment I discovered my own father was alive come rushing back, and I hope Jacob feels some fraction of that positive energy toward Odell.

When he lifts his head, tears are streaming down his cheeks. "I missed out on the first twenty-one years of your life, Mitzy. I thought no one could possibly know how that feels. But Odell has missed more than twice that many years of mine."

Throwing my arms around him, I hug him tight. "But he didn't, Dad. He was here the whole time. Odell was at your games, at community events, and he went to your high school graduation. He may have thought he was going because he was secretly still in love with Isadora, but, whatever the reason, he was there."

Jacob shakes with silent sobs, and I hold on to him and squeeze tighter. Several minutes pass before he disengages, wipes his face with his hands, and lets out a loud exhale. "Whew! We'll sure have something to talk about at that Christmas Eve supper!"

I bite my bottom lip and sit back.

"What? What did you do, Mitzy?"

"Oh, I invited Odell before I knew. And I re-invited him after I found out. But, I also told him about Grams."

"Oh boy, she's not going to be happy about that." Jacob snuffles and shakes his head. "Wow, honey. You've been a busy little elf."

"You mean, she *wasn't* happy about that. I told him, then I brought him up to the apartment, and I left them alone with a stack of 3 x 5 cards and a pen."

Relieved laughter shakes my father's barrel chest. "That's my girl. Well, I suppose we better break the news to the rest of the family."

Warmth spreads from my heart out to the tips of my fingers and toes. *The rest of the family.* I can't tell you how many times I sat in a social worker's office or a foster home, dreaming that there was a family out there somewhere that wanted me. My own family, that would love me and accept me, and maybe even buy me new clothes. Grams certainly has the clothing part covered!

My dad stands beside me, slowly waving a hand in front of my face. "Looks like I lost you. Are you coming with me for this dog-and-pony show or am I on my own?"

"Sorry, I was thinking about how lucky I am to have a family at all. And the fact that it's expanding . . . Bonus!"

He helps me up from the couch and swallows loudly. "I see it that way too, sweetie. If Cal was still alive, this might be more difficult to manage. But, as usual, your timing is exquisite."

I take a mock curtsy and follow him to the living room with a smile nearly splitting my face in two.

CHAPTER 20

WHEN JACOB and I emerge from the study, Amaryllis meets us with freshly topped up champagne flutes. "You're just in time! I want to make a toast."

My dad slips an arm around my shoulders and winks.

Amaryllis tosses her red-brown locks and raises her crystal ware. "To the best family I could have ever hoped to be part of, and to my favorite season of the year. Merry Christmas to my favorite husband, my favorite daughter, and my favorite son!"

We all clink glasses and take a sip of our champagne. Before Amaryllis can retire to the sofa, my father picks up where she left off. "I'd like to add to that."

Flecks of gold and green brighten her brown eyes and her smile sparkles.

Jacob inhales deeply and lifts his glass. "I'd like to make a toast to finding an amazing woman, who I surely don't deserve. And I'd like to make an additional toast to my snoopy daughter uncovering a wonderful family secret."

He moves to clink his glass to ours, but Amaryllis pulls her champagne back and wags a finger at him. "Oh, no you don't, Snugglebear. No one's acknowledging that toast until you spill the secret."

And now his wink makes perfect sense. Not only has he picked the right moment, but also, he's actually forced his audience to beg for the reveal. Maybe I get some of my smarts from him as well as my brilliant mama.

Jacob lifts his glass again and continues. "Turns out, Odell Johnson is my biological father. So here's to dads of all shapes, sizes, and origins. I've been blessed to have not one, but two great ones."

Before we can clink glasses, Stellen raises his higher and adds, "Me too."

Well, there's not a dry eye in the house when our glasses clink a second time.

And when Erick calls to tell me he's sorry he had to work late and can't cook for me, and can't pick up dinner because the diner is closed, I cry so hard I can't make the words. I'm trying to explain that I'm the reason the diner is closed, but—

My kind father gently takes my phone and invites Erick over for leftovers and an explanation.

A few minutes later, Erick shows up, concerned and confused.

But after Amaryllis fills his belly with her glorious food, and I work my way through half a box of tissue replaying the evening's emotional scenes, Erick is satisfied, in all the ways that matter.

We say our goodbyes and head back to his mom-free house. I won't bore you with the long list of things I love about Erick, but I'm definitely going to point out one of the top three.

This man has a heart the size of Texas, and even though we hardly ever have time to ourselves, he chooses to light a fire in his fireplace, make me a cup of cocoa, and snuggle up next to me on the sofa while I watch old Christmas classics and cry my eyes out.

"It's official, Erick Harper, you've earned yourself the 'Boyfriend of the Year' award. Now, the competition may be stiffer next year, so you might want to step up your game. However, for this year, you're a lock."

He removes the box of tissue from my lap, wipes a thumb across my cheek to remove a straggling tear, and envelops me in his safe, warm arms.

I'd be lying if I said things didn't take a delight-fully romantic turn, but there's no need to kiss and tell.

When the early morning sun breaks through his thin drapes, I have high hopes for a lazy breakfast and multiple cups of coffee.

Sheriff Harper has other plans. As he leans over to kiss me goodbye, already in his freshly pressed uniform, my heart sinks.

"Don't look so disappointed, Moon. There's sure to be a Christmas Eve encore." He winks.

My skin tingles underneath his old college sweatshirt. "Copy that."

His mouth may be saying he has to go to work, but his kiss is absolutely telling me he'd rather not.

"I'll see you for the big holiday supper tonight. Be careful out there, Sheriff."

Erick lunges at me, slips a hand under the covers, and tickles me mercilessly. "You be careful in here, Moon."

One last inhale of his citrus-woodsy scent and I collapse onto the pillow as he struts from the room and calls out a final warning. "No peeking at presents. And no *hunches*!"

"Cross my heart."

Everyone's working so hard to put our relation-ship on the fast track, but in moments like these, everything feels exactly as it should be.

Perfect.

Although, I can't believe he left me to my own devices for brekkie.

My skills in the kitchen produce one adequate pot of coffee and a measly bowl of cold cereal.

Myrtle's Diner is closed for the holiday. In fact, they shutter all eateries in town for at least the next two days.

Mmmmm. Cereal. Crunch. Crunch.

I wonder if—

Blerg. I gotta get out of this house or I can't be held responsible for what might happen to the prezzies under our no-tree.

The streets of Pin Cherry are oddly quiet, and grey clouds hang heavy over the great lake.

"Looks like snow." A phrase commonly heard around town. I'm fortunate to have a short commute to my holiday festivities this evening.

As I muse over my growing family, my heart goes out to Miss Tremblay, who will spend this Christmas alone. To be fair, Norma Olsen will probably spend the holiday alone too, since Niklas is sitting in a holding cell. However, I'm having trouble finding sympathy for that piece of the puzzle.

The bookshop looks inviting, despite the brewing storm, and I can't wait to put the finishing touches on Erick's present.

No sooner have I "put a bow on it" than—
BING. BONG. BING.

"Who could that be?"

Pye's uninterested grunt is my only reply.

Racing down the stairs, I open the door to a fabulous surprise. "What are you doing here?"

Erick dips his head in that way that insinuates he's doffing a cap and grins. "It's not that I don't trust you—"

"Hey, I'm not sure I like the way this is heading."

He scoops his arms around me, plants an eager smooch on my lips, and starts over. "What I meant to say is that I can't wait to give you your present. Plus, I think it makes more logistical sense to give it to you now, so you can tell everyone at supper."

My mood ring isn't offering any hints, but my tummy is tumbling like a load of laundry in a commercial dryer. I might panic. I'm not ready—

"Moon, are you going to invite me in, or do you want to open it in the middle of the alley?" His words are playful, but there seems to be some nervous concern lurking behind his eyes.

"Oh, right! Come in. I'll run up and grab yours. Be right back."

His mouth drops open, but I make my escape before he can protest.

My hair is still ninety-percent bedhead and I'm

wearing jeans and a tee. Is this the outfit I want to be wearing when it happens? If Grams— Get a hold of yourself, Moon.

Smacking myself firmly on the forehead, I pick up his brightly wrapped package, take a deep breath, and head out to the loft.

Erick is kneeling on the Persian rug, and I think my heart stopped beating!

"Wait! I'm not ready. I mean, I think it's what I want, but—"

He stands and scrunches up his face. "You're not ready for a present? How do you know if you want it? You don't know what it—"

I stop a couple paces from him and our eyes meet.

He looks at my face, glances back toward the floor, and points to the spot where he was kneeling. "Whoa! Did you think— Is that what you want?"

Rushing forward, I drop his gift on an oak reading table and wrap my arms around him. "Everyone keeps talking about next steps, and grandkids, and I kinda panicked."

He kisses the top of my head. "We're in charge of this relationship, Mitzy. We get to decide what next step feels right. I know surprise proposals are super romantic, but I'm not a gambling kind of guy. When—notice I'm not saying *if* —when we get there, we'll both know it's time."

I loosen my arms and tilt my head back.

His warm, blue eyes are brimming with love.

"Yeah. We're in charge. I like the sound of that."

Erick kisses me softly and whispers, "Do you want your present or not?"

Shoving the red-and-green package I just finished wrapping at him, I stall. "You first."

He tears the paper, opens the box, and laughs. "You got me a gun?"

Pointing at the weapon, I clarify. "I'm giving you my gun, or, rather, the gun I obtained. Pye and Grams insisted I get rid of it, and Silas said the Yule fire wasn't—"

His lips are on mine, and the rest of my speech evaporates. "Thanks, Moon. This is the nicest thing you could've possibly given me."

"Really? You like it?"

He chuckles. "It's no engagement ring, but it's a good next step."

"Touché."

His hand brushes mine and he passes me an envelope.

Schooling my features, I prepare to act like a gift card is a thoughtful gift. I paste on a smile, loosen the flap of the envelope, and slide out the card.

He's holding his breath as I read the inscription.

"Families and memories go hand in hand. Love you, Erick." I take the folded paper gift certificate from the card and smooth it open. "Oh, Erick!" Cue the waterworks!

His strong arms are around me in a flash. "I didn't want to tempt fate, but I figured once the initial shock wore off, your dad would be okay with the Odell situation. I thought maybe you'd like to get a family picture with your whole family. You know . . ."

"Thank you! This is such a wonderful idea. Pictures mean so much to me, since I lost all those memories in the foster system. Now I have a new, and expanding, family, and I can't wait to get some foolish pictures in matching sweaters—or some such nonsense."

Erick smiles. "You're welcome. And, I gotta get back to work if I plan to finish in time to make this supper gig." His lips brush my cheek and he heads down the spiral staircase.

Leaning over the thick banister, I call after him. "I'm calling next year's race. Erick Harper, 'Best Boyfriend' two years running!"

He chuckles, and the alley door thunks closed behind him.

And to think, I used to loathe the holidays.

CHAPTER 21

I'M NOT certain what sort of magic Amaryllis is working in the kitchen next door, but I swear I can smell the delicious aromas wafting across the alley.

With no one to distract me, this day threatens to be the longest in history.

My morning started far too early because of Erick racing off to work to complete all the reports surrounding the Carol Olsen homicide. And, despite the brief shimmering moment of perfection when we exchanged gifts, the ticking of the metaphorical clock is driving me mad.

Now, I'm lounging around my apartment hoping Grams forgives me for sharing her ghostly existence with her first husband, or at least appears to offer me some company and conversation.

But it's almost noon, and there's no sign of her.

Christmas Eve supper is scheduled for 5:30 p.m. sharp.

"When all else fails, it's time for the impossible."

Pyewacket is unimpressed with my announcement and flops a paw over his head to block my needy pontifications.

I toss on skinny jeans and a T-shirt that pictures a stack of books and reads "Never judge a book by its movie," and head next door.

When the elevator pings and the doors slide open, my father and Stellen look at me with desperation widening their eyes, while Amaryllis is as cheery as ever. "Mitzy! Come on in. I can always use an extra pair of hands in the kitchen."

Quickly taking in the scene, I wink at the boys. "Do you think we can get rid of these two? I was hoping we could have a little girl time."

She stops in the middle of the kitchen and wells up with emotion. "Oh, Mitzy, that would be so wonderful." Picking up a dishtowel, she flicks it at my father's behind. "You get on out of here. I'm sure you and Stellen can find a car to work on or a gun to clean. Leave this meal preparation to the women."

I'm not entirely sure I agree with her gender stereotypes, but when I see the look of relief on my father's face and receive a thankful finger gun from my stepbrother, I'm happy to take one for the team.

"Do you need an apron?" She adjusts her red-brown curls and tightens her high-pony.

No one has ever asked me that question in the kitchen in my lifetime. "I don't think so. And I should probably offer you fair warning. I'm not great in the kitchen. I heat things up in a microwave, I make a decent cup of coffee, and that's pretty much where the list ends."

Slipping an arm around my shoulders, she hugs me conspiratorially. "Nonsense. You're smart as a whip. I'll have you ready for *The Great British Baking Show* in no time!"

Yeesh. This woman is going to suffer the disappointment of a lifetime today.

"I'll let you work on the mince pies. Just cut the butter into the flour, to form a crumbly meal, and then press it into a ball. We'll need to let that refrigerate while you work on the filling."

My feet remain firmly planted in the middle of the kitchen.

Amaryllis notices my lack of motion and tilts her head to the side. "Have you never made piecrust, dear?"

Scrunching up my face, I avoid the question. "I can pick a lock with my eyes closed, I can hot-wire a

car, and I can lift a wallet without drawing attention nine times out of ten."

She rushes across the kitchen and envelops me
in a motherly embrace. "I'm so sorry, Mitzy. How
stupid of me. Here I was planning this whole
British Christmas supper menu in honor of your
mother, and it never occurred to me that she died
before she had a chance to pass on her knowledge
of cooking."

Far be it from me to break the news to
Amaryllis that my mother was no chef. She was indeed British, and she kept my belly full, by hook or
by crook, every day until she left this earth, but she
was no Mary Berry. "Don't worry about it. I never
had much use for cooking. The other skills have
served me a lot better over the years, but I suppose I
should figure out how to make dinner for Erick at
least once."

Loosening her arms, she grips both of my hands
tightly. "Oh, Mitzy. You two make the most
adorable couple! I just want things to work out. Is it
wrong of me to hope for an engagement? Of course,
not right now. But maybe next year? He's just the
most wonderful guy. And I see in his face how
much he loves you."

Boy, this woman is not one to hide her emotions. If I tell her about the kerfuffle that just went
down in the Rare Books Loft, she will faint.

"Things are really great between us. And I'm happy with the speed at which the relationship is moving. I'm not going to jinx anything by making wishes or promises."

She shakes my hands up and down before releasing them. "Good point. Good point. Never look a gift horse in the mouth, my mother used to say."

Amaryllis gestures sweepingly to her well-appointed kitchen. "Today is cooking 101. I'm going to teach you all the basics, and when we sit down to supper with the family, I hope you feel as good as I do about making a wonderful meal for people you love."

"I hope so too." Secretly, I'm not sure what I hope, but I know that I don't plan to spend an entire day in the kitchen and have people regret it. So it's time to put on my pay-attention hat and make my moves count.

This woman is so organized it's a little frightening.

"Here's the menu. We're having roast turkey and cranberry-glazed ham. I know I should have simply picked one, but the leftovers last forever, and who isn't going to like more options?"

Sensing this is a rhetorical question, I keep my thoughts to myself.

"Then we'll have oven-roasted red potatoes, and—I had a hard time deciding on the stuffing—

but I think I'm going to go with rye bread croutons and my sage and onion recipe. That seems like it will go nicely with turkey or ham."

Again, I don't feel my input is necessary.

"We're definitely making pigs in blankets and Yorkshire pudding. I know those are super popular in Great Britain. I'm sure your mother made them for you."

I seem to remember some kind of swine in a coverlet, but, if memory serves, they were hot dogs wrapped in ready-made dough from a can. Based on the swanky level of ingredients I see displayed on the counter, I don't think that's where Amaryllis is going.

"Of course, there will be gravy, cranberry sauce, and Brussels sprouts roasted with bacon! I know people have very strong opinions about Brussels sprouts, but trust me, this preparation is fabulous."

Just like my mom taught me, I nod and smile.

"And for dessert, we'll have Christmas pudding and mince pies. I couldn't decide between a traditional Christmas pudding or a figgy pudding, but when I was at the grocery store looking for ingredients, they didn't have any figs that met my standards, so I went with the Christmas pudding. That's already finished and soaking in brandy. I'm going to light it on fire when I serve it!"

Dear Lord baby Jesus! I didn't realize I would need utensils and a fire extinguisher for this meal.

"And last but not least, the mince pies. Maybe I already said that? Anyway, I think we might serve that with vanilla ice cream for anyone who's interested. What do you think?"

The habit of not answering sort of took over, and I fail to respond.

"Mitzy? Did I overwhelm you? Let's just take it one step at a time. By the end of the day you'll be surprised how much you've accomplished and how easy it really is."

"Copy that." I suppose I only have her word to take for it.

After doing as much damage as Amaryllis could accommodate in her kitchen, I hustle back to my apartment to endure Ghost-ma's wardrobe selection.

"Grams? Grams?"

Pyewacket allows his large head to loll off the side of the bed and stares through disinterested, upside-down golden eyes.

"Where's Grams? I haven't seen her since she and Odell— Well, you know."

He squeezes his eyelids closed and offers a complacent, "Reow." Can confirm.

Once more, with feeling. "Grams, I know you're upset with me, and I'm sorry that I spilled your ghostly beans to Odell. But the man is my grandfather! He deserves to be a part of our family, and I know we can trust him with our secrets. I hope you'll embrace the spirit of the season and forgive me. But in the meantime it looks like I'll have to pick out my own holiday outfit."

If that sentiment doesn't bring her ghost blasting through a wall, then I'm all out of options.

No ghost. No blasting.

However, the upside is I won't be teetering across the icy alley in a five-inch pair of Manolo Blahniks!

No sooner have the words formed in my mind than Myrtle Isadora snaps to life right in front of me.

"Yikes! You haven't scared me like that in quite a while."

A smug look curves one side of her mouth. "You deserve more than a fright. You had no right!"

"Are we speaking in rhymes now? Am I to sing my plea somehow?"

She floats toward me and her semi-corporeal fingers brush my cheek. "I can never stay mad at you. I do wish you had talked to me before you dragged Odell into this, but I'm glad he knows about you—and Jacob."

Due to my extreme maturity, I stop myself from chanting "told you so." Of course, simply thinking it means that Ghost-ma already got the message.

"Don't be a sore winner, Mizithra."

"I love you, Grams. And I'm glad you trusted me with the information, and I promise to be less impulsive in the future."

She hoots and hollers like a guest star on *Hee Haw* and slaps her ring-adorned hand on her designer gown. "You should take that show on the road, dear." Regaining her composure, she circles the massive closet, tapping a finger on her lip. "Let's see. What goes with the six-inch Jimmy Choo platforms?"

"Isadora! If you have any hope of having great-grandchildren, you better keep me in a shoe that won't kill me when I try to walk across the alley."

She stops, turns, and clutches her pearls. "What did you say? Did he ask? Let me see the ring!"

"Down, ghost, down. Like I've said more times than I can count, to more people than I care to mention, Erick and I have a wonderful relationship that is moving at the perfect pace. Do not pressure me. However, if you would like to win some potential great-ghost-mother brownie points, find me a two-inch heel."

The mere mention of great-grandchildren has her bubbling with excitement. No fewer than ten different outfits are tossed upon the padded mahogany bench.

Considering the brisk weather, I negotiate for a tailored pair of lined, grey wool pants and a refined, understated holiday sweater. This is not the kind of sweater that's going to win any hilarious contests. This is an elegant celebration of the season.

Once I switch into the new outfit, Grams insists I freshen my makeup and do something about my hair.

"Well, you can't wear a sophisticated outfit like that when your hair looks like something the cat dragged in."

"Reeeee-ow." A warning.

My eyes widen, and I shake a finger at Grams. "You better be careful. Thou shalt not take thy royal feline's name in vain!"

She chuckles and drifts off to scratch her ethereal fingers between Pyewacket's black-tufted ears.

A twist here and there with my styling wand and a spritz or three of hairspray, and I'm presentable.

"I'm sorry you can't come to Christmas Eve supper, but at least you're not spending it in a jail cell like Niklas Olsen."

Grams floats toward the window and her silly mood turns somber. "Tell everyone I wished them a Happy Christmas."

"A Happy Christmas? Are you British now? Before you answer that, I must inform you that Amaryllis planned the entire menu around traditional British dishes because she was sure that's what my mother would've served me."

Isadora presses a hand to her ample bosom. "Oh, that woman is absolutely the sweetest thing. I hope you didn't tell her your mother wasn't a cook."

"I didn't. Believe it or not, I've learned a thing or two about etiquette from a certain uppity ghost."

Before she can complete her retort, I slip out of the apartment, race down the stairs—even risking a holiday hop over the chain at the bottom of the staircase.

St. Nick smiles upon me, and I land safely on the ground floor.

When the elevator delivers me to the penthouse suite, the festive table is set with my stepmother's exquisite flair, and pretty much everyone has arrived. Twiggy and Wayne took a rain check and hopped on a plane to Mexico. They'd had quite enough of the weather and the murder accusations.

Silas, clad in an uncharacteristic green-and-red sweater vest, is braving winter's chill on the back deck with Stellen. They're deep in conversation as they puff on their cigars. You don't have to be psychic to see that my stepbrother, despite giving it the old college try, is green around the gills.

Boisterous voices in the den alert me to Erick's arrival. He and my father seem to be having an animated discussion of some sports team's something or other. Before I report to the kitchen for whatever duties Amaryllis has planned, I poke my head in and pass on Isadora's message. "She said to wish you all a Happy Christmas."

Jacob tilts his head. "So she's British now?"

I shrug. "This is what I'm saying. I think she must have an afterlife sense of smell that somehow helped her decipher this 'all UK' menu. She wishes she could be here, and that's her way of butting in, I suppose."

Erick leans back, cups a hand over his mouth, and whispers to my father. "Must run in the family."

Instantly planting a fist on my hip, I narrow my gaze. "I heard that, *Ricky*. I'd step lightly if I were you. Your mother has told me a few juicy tidbits that I don't think you would like me to share at dinner."

The sound of his mother's pet name for him, and my thinly veiled threat, do the trick.

He sits up straighter and nods comically. "Whatever you say, Miss Moon."

Jacob chuckles. "That's a smart man."

Following my stepmother's orders like a ready-made Stepford wife, I deliver all the lovely dishes to the table, and round up the menfolk.

Lively conversation and cross talk abound as we pass the delicious dishes around the table.

When the elevator pings, almost no one notices.

No one but me.

Odell Johnson steps into the penthouse with hesitant discomfort. His grey buzz cut glistens with a hint of some type of hair product, and re-placing his well-worn denim shirt is a red-and-green plaid flannel button-up that looks brand-new.

Nearly spilling the roasted Brussels sprouts with bacon, I shove my chair back and get to my feet. "Odell!"

A hush falls over the room, and all heads turn.

He swallows, and his Adam's apple makes a vis-ible struggle of it. "I brought a pie. Hope that's okay."

As I take a step toward the door, my father pushes his chair back and motions for me to sit down.

No one speaks. Platters of food seem to hover in midair.

Jacob approaches the man who simply used to hold the title of one of Isadora's ex-husbands and local diner owner, and nods toward the counter.

Odell places the pie on the granite surface and waits for further instruction.

My father's hands are shoved deep in his pockets. Their voices are low, and my normal sense of hearing can't pick up the details. At least I know enough to avoid invading their privacy with my extra senses.

Heads nod, shoulders shrug, and finally my father offers his hand to the man who gave him life.

Odell grips my father's hand and fights to keep his emotions buried behind his well-lined face.

Jacob lifts his other hand, pats Odell on the back, and gestures to the empty seat between Stellen and me.

I don't possess the subdued talents of my father or grandfather. When Odell gets near the table, I launch myself at him, wrap my arms around his neck and squeeze. "Let me know when you're ready for me to start calling you Gramps."

My silly comment does the trick, and a warm chuckle escapes as his shoulders relax.

He holds my chair for me and then takes a seat.

The platters resume their circuit, and everyone's plate is overflowing with holiday fare.

Silas and Amaryllis valiantly keep the conversation light and flowing until chairs are pushed back from the table and we rub our full bellies.

Seems like the perfect time for a break. I tap

Odell on the back and motion for him to follow me. We step toward the bank of windows that face my apartment across the alley. I've never tried to send Grams a message from this sort of distance, at least not with any success. But here goes. *Isadora, if you can hear me, please come to the window and wave a 3 x 5 card at us, so Odell knows you're there.*

To his credit, he waits patiently beside me without making a sound.

Just when I think my efforts are in vain, a small index card appears in the window, sliding back and forth, displaying a beautiful heart-shape drawn by my grandmother.

Odell sniffles and wipes a weathered thumb under each eye. "Like I said, best Christmas present ever."

He slips an arm around my shoulders and I lean my head toward him. "You're welcome, Gramps."

End of Book 16

A NOTE FROM TRIXIE

Woot! Odell is finally in the inner circle—and another case solved! I'll keep writing them if you keep reading . . .

The best part of "living" in Pin Cherry Harbor continues to be feedback from my early readers. Thank you to my alpha readers/cheerleaders, Angel and Michael. HUGE thanks to my fantastic beta readers who continue to give me extremely useful and honest feedback: Veronica McIntyre and Nadine Peterse-Vrijhof. And big "small town" hugs to the world's best ARC Team – Trixie's Mystery ARC Detectives!

I always appreciate the insightful edits of my no-nonsense editor Philip Newey. I'd also like to give a heaping helping of gratitude to Brooke for her tireless proofreading! (Despite her busy schedule.) Any errors are my own, as my outdated version of Word insists on showing me only what it likes and when it feels so moved.

I'm especially grateful for the helpful guns, silencers, and ammunition info provided by Morgan.

FUN FACT: I have had the pleasure of picking and cutting my own Yule tree more than ten times! Full disclosure, several of those trips involved lengthy snowball fights.

My favorite line from this case: "For the record, it's a cover story, not a secret identity. I'm a snoop, not a superhero." ~Mitzy

I'm currently writing book seventeen in the Mitzy Moon Mysteries series, and I think I may just live in Pin Cherry Harbor forever. Mitzy, Grams, and Pyewacket got into plenty of trouble in book one, *Fries and Alibis*. But I'd have to say that book three, *Wings and Broken Things*, is when most readers say the series becomes unputdownable.

I hope you'll continue to hang out with us.

Trixie Silvertale (November 2021)

DANGERS AND EMPTY MANGERS

Mitzy Moon Mysteries No. 17

A frozen cheesemaker. A vandalized Nativity. Can our psychic sleuth serve up justice before she's iced?

Mitzy Moon might be getting too comfortable. Her love life is satisfying, her family is supportive, and her extra senses are becoming more reliable. But, before she can bask in that glow, a suspicious death and a missing Messiah threaten to spoil the New Year...

Sniffing out the murderer of a local cheese-maker should be her guiding star, but there's nothing as upsetting as a stolen baby Jesus. And with the trail growing smellier than a ripe Limburger, she's desperate for help from her supernatural supporting cast. Unfortunately, with her powers now leading her in circles, she may have to make the ultimate sacrifice.

Can Mitzy peel the rind off the culprit before she's prematurely aged?

Dangers and Empty Mangers is the seventeenth book in the hilarious paranormal cozy mystery series, Mitzy Moon Mysteries. If you like snarky heroines, supernatural misfits, and a dash of romance, then you'll love Trixie Silvertale's heartfelt whodunits.

Buy *Dangers and Empty Mangers* to curdle a killer today!

Grab yours here!
readerlinks.com/l/861835

Scan this QR Code with the camera on your phone. You'll be taken right to the Mitzy Moon Mysteries series page. You can easily grab any mysteries you've missed!

Once you're in the Club, you'll also be the first to receive updates from Pin Cherry Harbor and access to giveaways, new release announcements, behind-the-scenes secrets, and much more!

Scan this QR Code with the camera on your phone. You'll be taken right to the page to join the Club!

THANK YOU!

Trying out a new book is always a risk and I'm thankful that you rolled the dice with Mitzy Moon. If you loved the book, the sweetest thing you can do (*even sweeter than pin cherry pie à la mode*) is to leave a review so that other readers will take a chance on Mitzy and the gang.

Don't feel you have to write a book report. A brief comment like, "Can't wait to read the next book in this series!" will help potential readers make their choice.

★★★★★
Leave a quick review HERE
ttps://readerlinks.com/l/1920569
★★★★★

Thank you kindly, and I'll see you in Pin Cherry Harbor!

More to come!

ABOUT THE AUTHOR

Trixie Silvertale grew up reading an endless supply of Lilian Jackson Braun, Hardy Boys, and Nancy Drew novels. She loves the amateur sleuths in cozy mysteries and obsesses about all things paranormal. Those two passions unite in her Mitzy Moon Mysteries, and she's thrilled to write them and share them with you.

When she's not consumed by writing, she bakes to fuel her creative engine and pulls weeds in her herb garden to clear her head (*and sometimes she pulls out her hair, but mostly weeds*).

Greetings are welcome:
trixie@trixiesilvertale.com

BB bookbub.com/authors/trixie-silvertale

f facebook.com/TrixieSilvertale

O instagram.com/trixiesilvertale

Manufactured by Amazon.ca
Bolton, ON

26884496R00155